Adam

CHRIS KENISTON

USA TODAY BESTSELLING AUTHOR

Indie House Publishing

Copyright © 2016 Christine Baena

Indie House Publishing

BOOKS BY CHRIS KENISTON

Aloha Series
Aloha Texas
Almost Paradise
Mai Tai Marriage
Dive Into You
Shell Game
Look of Love
Love by Design
Love Walks In
Waikiki Wedding

Surf's Up Flirts
(Aloha Series Companions)
Shall We Dance
Love on Tap
Head Over Heels
Perfect Match
Just One Kiss
It Had to Be You

Honeymoon Series
Honeymoon for One
Honeymoon for Three

Family Secrets Novels
Champagne Sisterhood
The Homecoming
Hope's Corner

ACKNOWLEDGEMENTS

Transitioning from beach locations to west Texas ranch country can be a bit challenging for a born-and-bred city girl. Especially one who has never been around cattle.

To pull this off, I needed help from a great many people. I have to thank my good friends Lindsey McKenna and J. M. Madden, who kept me from doing something really stupid with the animals in the barn!

I thank my son, James, for attending school in that part of the state, so I at least have some idea what a real cowboy looks like or what it means to have dinner at the only restaurant in town!

And, at the end of my rope, when the characters stop talking to me, I have S. E. Smith to thank for brainstorming with me until the end was in sight.

Y'all rock!

CHAPTER ONE

S hooting the cheating, conniving sleazebag between the eyes wasn't the best idea she'd ever had. After all, Texas was a death penalty state. On the other hand, a well-placed bullet in each ball could work. Didn't Lorena Bobbitt get off scot-free?

Margaret Colleen O'Brien glanced at the clock on the dashboard. She'd driven through the night, conjuring up the most satisfying ways to get even with Jonathan J. Cox. So far shooting his balls off was number one on her list.

• • •

Adam Farraday folded his tired body into the driver's seat of his pickup truck. Long nights like this—with no time for sleep—were an absolute killer, but, when the fates were on his side, the elation on the mornings after were beyond the best. Or, in this case, near morning. At six thirty the sun barely winked over the horizon. He had just enough time to make it back to town for a quick shower, change of clothes, another gallon of coffee and the last piece of his aunt Eileen's cinnamon crumb cake before his first appointment of the day.

Or not.

The car on the side of the road ahead was sleek, red, low-to-the-ground and tilting to one side. What moron drove a car like that in this lonely part of the country in the middle of the night? He could see it now: a retired balding lawyer, looking to rekindle his youth behind the wheel of a speed-trap-finding red sports car. And, if that wasn't enough, the idiot had to do it in west Texas cattle country.

So much for the shower and crumb cake. By the time Adam

changed the tire for the man—who probably didn't even know where to find the spare—Adam would be lucky to get to work on time. He pulled off the two-lane road, mumbling to himself. "God, spare me from stupid city people."

Parking a few yards behind the stranded sports car, he hadn't yet had time to turn off the ignition when the fire-engine-red driver's side door opened. And an angel in white stepped out.

He blinked twice, deciding he wasn't hallucinating. The vision before him was most definitely not a balding lawyer suffering from a midlife crisis. A stunning redhead in a flowing gown stood stiffly, hanging on to the edge of the car door.

Stepping from the cab of his truck, he moved in her direction. She offered a shaky smile, and he noticed her grip on the door tightened. Standing six foot four, at the break of dawn, on a deserted backcountry highway, he could probably scare the life out of anyone, even an angel. Except this angel had no wings. She was all woman.

The closer he got, the more he could see her features. Eyes such a deep bright blue he could make out the shade even in the dim morning light. Hair cropped just above her shoulders shone with natural highlights from the sun. Another step and he saw even more clearly. His angel wasn't just a woman. She was a bride.

What was left of a veil hung slightly off-kilter, and, from the dark mascara smears on her cheeks, he didn't expect to find a groom anywhere nearby.

"Looks like you're having a little trouble."

Her brows shot up, and those bright blue eyes flashed stormy gray. "Ya think?"

He considered apologizing, though he wasn't sure what for, but opted to ignore the attitude and just deal with the car. The sooner she was on her way, the sooner he could get that shower he so desperately wanted. "Have you got a spare?"

"In the trunk."

He veered toward the front of the midengine car, while the pretty angel with the fiery tongue reached inside the vehicle for the key fob and popped the trunk. It took him all of thirty seconds to shift around the few things inside, including the one bag she had, pull out the spare, bounce it off the ground and recognize trouble. "Sorry, ma'am, but when was the last time you checked the air in this tire?"

Those same brows that shot to her hairline minutes ago curled into a sharp V; then she blew out a loud sigh. "It's not my car."

Ookaay. A snippy bride in a stolen car. A disabled stolen car. What a way to start what was clearly going to be a very long day. He pulled off his hat, slapped it against his thigh and drew in a long, deep breath.

"It's his," she said, her voice small. Not so fierce anymore. A glimmer of tears pooled in her eyes, seconds before she blinked them back and drew herself upright again. In control again. "A dog."

Adam let his gaze roam from the top of her head down to her toes, pausing for a brief second at her well-displayed cleavage, before settling his attention back on her face. "At least he has good taste."

The momentary flare of temper that flashed at his checking her out slid behind an expression of utter confusion. "What?"

"He has good taste in, uh, cars."

"The dog?"

"If you say so." Though his first thought was anyone who let a looker like this get away was probably an idiot too. "I can give you a ride into town, take the spare. Ned'll patch up the tire and bring you back here."

She shook her head. "I'm waiting for daylight. I have to find him."

Adam cast a quick glance around them. All he could see was miles of west Texas dirt. "Who?"

"The dog!" she snapped. "I have to find him. Or her."

Or her? "Ma'am, it's been a long night. I'm in desperate need of caffeine, and I have a full day ahead of me. Exactly what are you talking about?"

"The dog." She waved her arm at the surrounding landscape. "He—or she—came out of nowhere and just ran in front of me. That's when I swerved, blew a tire and wound up parked on the side of this godforsaken road. I must have hit or run over someth … Oh, God." She leaned against the car. "You don't think I hit him, do you? I mean, I'd know it, wouldn't I?"

He had no time to muster a reply, as his vision in white had pushed away from the car and darted off in search of … a dog. If someone's dog had wandered this far away from home, and she had hit him, causing her to run off the road, the animal could be curled up behind a rock, licking his wounds and slowly dying of internal injuries. Damn. The circle of life.

"Hang on," he called.

His angel in white had already hiked up her dress and flung the layers of fabric over one arm. For all the good it did her, as four-inch heels were not acceptable hiking shoes. At least the dry Texas clay was hard as rock, or the lady would be sinking with every step, like a golf tee. Her only potential risk would be breaking an ankle.

He reached for her arm to hold her still. "What kind of dog are we looking for?"

"I don't know." Her gaze scanned the area again. "Not small. Maybe medium size or a little bigger. Fluffy tail. You know, not a skinny tail like a Lab. Dark fur. At least I think so. I don't know." Tears pooled in her eyes again, and she swiped at her cheeks with her bare hand.

"You know what?" Adam pulled a handkerchief from his breast pocket and handed it to her. "Sounds to me like maybe you saw a coyote."

In an instant her tearful expression shifted to mild alarm. "A coyote?"

He bit back a smile. "They're real common in these parts, and, if that's what you saw, he's probably long gone and just fine. But …" He raised his hand to stop her from making any objections. "Just in case, you're going to sit in my truck—before you break your neck stomping around in those shoes—while I take a quick scan of the area and make sure we don't have an injured dog to deal with."

The vision in white opened her mouth, no doubt to argue, but didn't quite have enough time. Not wanting to deal with an injured dog *and* a woman with a broken ankle, Adam scooped her into his arms like a groom prepared to carry his bride over the threshold or, in this case, to deposit her in the safety of his truck.

He buried the smile that threatened to spring at her squeal of surprise—then suppressed the stream of words that came to mind as she whacked him repeatedly on the shoulder.

"Put me down!" she shouted.

"In another second."

"For God's sake, I can walk!" Legs now flailing like scissors gone mad, she hammered at him again, then pushed away and screeched loud enough for every breathing being from here to El Paso to hear. "I said, put me down!"

To prevent her from pounding on him again, he flung her over his shoulder, yanked open the truck door and, as gently as possible with 110 pounds of squirming woman, deposited her in the seat. "I'll get my bag and go look for our coyote. You stay put."

Bone tired, he was what his aunt Eileen would call dead and too dumb to fall over, but, if his misguided bride was right, and an injured dog was out there somewhere, he had to find it.

Much to his surprise, his otherwise-very-vocal bride sat in silence as he opened the back door of the quad cab, and pulled out a stethoscope.

"There!" She waved an arm and flew out of the truck. "Oh, he's limping."

"Stop." Adam stuck out his arm and grabbed her, before she ran off and broke her neck chasing after a who-knew-what. "I'll go. You stay put."

In the distance he saw a slow-moving shadow. Too big for a coyote. Damn. She was right. Somehow a dog had wound up out here in the middle of nowhere. Adam hunched down and whistled low, then called, "Here, boy."

The dog lifted his head, and, if Adam didn't know better, he'd swear the dog nodded at him, before turning and walking away.

"Oh, he's leaving!" Again she stepped forward, clearly ready to sprint after the dog. And once more he had to reach out and turn her about. "Really, miss, would you *please* let me go after him?"

She spun around in the direction of the dog. "But he's ..."

Her words trailed off, and Adam followed her glance. The dog was gone. The nearest crop of rocks for him to hide behind was too far off in the distance. No way had he made it that far in just the few seconds it had taken for them to turn around and back again. "Stay here. Please," he repeated.

Lips pressed tightly together, she nodded at him, then whispered softly, "Hurry, please."

The sun rose higher in the sky, casting a warm light across the dry Texas dirt. More than looking for the dog, Adam searched for something the dog could use for shelter. But there wasn't a blessed thing large enough to hide anything the size of the animal he'd seen moments ago. He'd reached the spot where he'd seen the dog. No paw prints. No tracks. He hadn't imagined him. They'd both seen the animal. He had to be here somewhere. Didn't he?

A few feet farther, Adam stopped to look back. He could no longer see the expression on the bride's face, but he could feel the intensity with which she watched him and the barren land around him. Probably jilted on her wedding day, definitely stranded in the middle of west Texas cattle country, yet her only concern was for an injured dog. He'd have to cut this city girl a little slack. Even if she did want to stomp about in four-inch heels and a wedding gown.

Surveying the empty land around him, Adam blew out a fast clip of short repetitive whistles and waited. Nothing. No sign of any four-legged creatures. "Okay, fellow. How did you get out here in the first place? And where the hell have you gone to now?"

CHAPTER TWO

Okay, now what? Meg stood in the cramped little bathroom at the back of the garage. Considering how long she'd coveted the prized Vera Wang wedding gown that sat in a heap on the dirty floor, she wondered how dangerous it would be if she lit a match to it and watched the expensive dress go up in flames, like the rest of her life. She hadn't wanted the elaborate over-the-top wedding her mother and Jonathan had agreed on, but she had so loved the dress.

"You okay, miss?" Ned, the wiry old mechanic—who she'd swear had been around since the Model T—called to her.

Was she okay? The man she'd trusted with her heart and soul—and bank account—was a lying cheat. Every time her mind wandered back to standing at the gas pump and seeing her credit card denied—only to call and discover their spectacular first-class European honeymoon had been bought and paid for with her now maxed-out Visa card—she remembered why shooting the slime bucket in the balls was such a satisfying solution.

"Miss? If I'm gonna go look at that snazzy car of yours, I need to go now."

She glanced down quickly at the cotton shirt and capris she wore and hoped they didn't look too much like what they were—something she'd worn yesterday before changing into her gown. Quickly shoving the gown into the trash, she grabbed the doorknob and yanked it open. "I'm ready. Let's go." The inside of the tow truck wasn't in any better shape than the bathroom she'd used to change her clothes. Ignoring the seats held together with duct tape and avoiding the miscellaneous grease spots scattered about, Meg slid into the cab.

"You sure are lucky Doc Adam was out at the Thomas ranch.

If you ask me, old man Jake takes better care of those prize horses of his than he does his own family. Yes siree, good for you the doc was out there for the birthing of one of those foals, or you could have been sitting out on that lonely road for hours, maybe days."

Meg nodded. She hadn't said much from the moment she'd been dropped off at the garage, changed from bride-to-be to single woman and climbed into this truck with a character straight out of Andy Griffith's fictional Mayberry. She hadn't had to. Ned, the geriatric mechanic, who Adam had assured her could fix anything with an engine, had done most of the talking.

Even when he asked a question, he didn't give her time to answer before moving on with his conversation. And a good thing too. Right now she needed answers of her own.

The analog clock on the dashboard told her it was already eight o'clock. It had taken nearly forty minutes to get to town from where the car had broken down. Another few minutes for the mechanic and veterinarian to do their country good-morning routine while she changed out of her wedding gown. Now, scanning the dusty horizon in search of that stupid car, she wondered how the hell to fix the mess her world had become.

One thing she knew for sure. She couldn't go back. Not to Dallas. That decision had been made somewhere west of Fort Worth, about the same time she'd disconnected the GPS, tossed her cell phone out the window and driven over it. Twice.

"Good stock, those Farradays." Ned's voice drifted past her thoughts. "Six boys. And they don't come much prettier than their sister, Grace."

Meg blinked. She had no idea what the man was talking about.

"Shame about Helen. Good woman. She'd be mighty proud of her little girl."

Her mind scrambled to follow the thread of conversation. Farraday? Wasn't that the cowboy veterinarian's last name? Yes, Adam Farraday. Once they'd given up on searching for the missing dog, they'd exchanged names. He'd barely finished assuring her the local mechanic was more than qualified to resolve her car trouble when she'd fallen asleep on the drive into town.

"Here we are." Ned climbed out of the tow truck and ambled over to the car, looking more like a man who had spent his life on a horse than holding a socket wrench. "We'll fix that tire first. Then I'll take a look under the hood."

Meg hit the fob to release the trunk. With nothing to do but wait, she looked around in the light of day. The view was not much better than it had been at night. The only thing as far as her eye could see was dirt, dust, and more dirt. Was it possible for everything on the horizon to be scarecrow yellow? Surely there should be some color somewhere. A green shrub, a brown cow, a painted horse. Something?

And where had that dog gone? In her favorite Anne Klein loafers, she considered walking to the nearest cluster of big rocks to search again for any sign of the injured animal but put aside the thought. If he'd been nearby, they would have found him earlier this morning. But still she wondered.

"I hope you're not in any hurry." Ned wiped his hands on a rag and slammed the hood of the car shut.

"What's wrong?"

"You blew more than a tire. That puddle of water under there? Probably hit a rock 'cause your radiator's leaking. I'll have to get it on a rack to make sure there are no other problems with the linkage to the wheel."

Even not knowing a damn thing about cars, with the way her luck had been running, she'd be willing to bet none of this would be a cheap fix. "How much will that cost?"

Ned closed an eye and glanced upward. With every second that ticked by, her frazzled nerves nudged the urge to shoot someone up another notch.

"Like I said, I won't know for sure till I get a good look-see under her belly, but parts won't be cheap. If a regular radiator costs about $300, one for this foreign baby is probably gonna cost you at least $1,200, maybe more, and that's just for parts."

Twelve hundred? It might as well be twelve thousand. Stuck out in the middle of nowhere with no money, no job, no car and no life. Damn you, Jonathan Cox.

● ● ●

"Don't you look like something the cat dragged in." Becky Wilson stood five foot four and weighed in light enough for Adam to pick up with one arm. Though twelve years his junior, with long blonde hair and bangs that made her look even younger, she ran Adam's animal clinic with the same iron hand her grandmother had run it for Doc Simmons before him. No one would dare contradict her.

"Good morning to you too." After spending almost an hour with sleeping beauty, and no time to shower after pulling an all-nighter at the Thomas ranch, his sparse retort was the best he could manage.

One hundred years ago the original incarnation of this old homestead had been the closest ranch to town. Fifty years ago the town limits had spread to its front doorstep, and, rather than see it torn down, Doc Simmons bought it. Single at the time, he'd remodeled the second floor into living quarters and converted the ground floor into the veterinary clinic. The old barn was saved for the large animal center. Since buying the place from Doc Simmons, Adam had hired a specialized equine tech and receptionist in addition to the existing main clinic tech and office manager. He was damn proud of his reputation and the clinic's growth.

The main wing wasn't very big, but, on mornings like today, the walk down the hall to Adam's office felt interminable. His first appointment was due in a few minutes—a golden retriever in for an annual checkup. If Adam hurried, he'd have just enough time for a quick cup of java and some of the cheese crackers stashed in his desk drawer.

Rounding the corner, he skidded to a stop. A cup of hot black coffee and a piece of his aunt Eileen's crumb cake sat on his desk. Steam rising from the dark mug, he marveled for the umpteenth time at Becky's uncanny sense of timing.

His first sip of the warm brew went a long way toward making him feel human again. After a bite of the savory crumb cake, he was ready to get down on bended knee and kiss Becky's feet.

"Poured the coffee when I heard you pull into the lot." Her impeccable timing unmarred, Becky stood in his doorway, arms folded, a Cheshire cat grin on her face.

"Thank you." He took another long swallow. "Will you marry me?"

"It would be under false pretenses. I'd love to take credit for the cake, but your aunt dropped it off on her way to the Silver Spurs. Besides, Sally May would never forgive me."

Sally May Henderson was somewhere close to either side of sixty, and every time she brought her German shepherd, Rabb, into the clinic, she'd tease Adam mercilessly about him being too good-looking and her being too short, too old or too married. She kidded around that way with all the Farraday brothers.

"Heard you picked up a passenger this morning." Becky unfolded her arms and stepped into his office.

Munching on the last bite of cake, he arched a questioning brow.

Becky shrugged. "Hey, by 7:00 a.m., downtown Tuckers Bluff is a thriving metropolis."

"Thriving metropolis?"

"Okay, my grandmother saw you driving up Main Street and called."

"Lady had a flat on the old farm road. She thought she hit a dog."

Becky's eyes rounded with concern as she glanced over his shoulder and out the window. "Where is he?"

"Good question. One minute he was limping away, and the next minute he was gone."

"Damn. Is he in your truck still?"

Not having enough caffeine in his system yet, it took Adam a few moments to process the question. "No, not *dead* gone. *Gone* as in *vanished*."

"Did you drink some of old man Thomas' homemade hooch?"

The question begged for an indignant defense, but he was too tired to even bother rolling his eyes at her. Instead he closed them, pinched the bridge of his nose and on a heavy sigh mumbled, "No."

Becky studied him with eyes wiser than her young years warranted. "Want me to call D.J., see if he can spare someone to go look?"

Adam shook his head. Had the dog been there to find, he'd have found him. And besides, he'd have to call his brother the police chief on another matter. One red, possibly stolen, very expensive sports car. "Have we gotten the labs back on Mrs. Quinn's cat?"

"Not yet."

The door chime dinged the arrival of their first patient. With the synchronization of a practiced routine, Becky hurried back to her post as Adam pushed away from his desk, prepared for the long day ahead of him. If, at the end of the day, he wasn't ready to drop with a strong wind, maybe he'd go back and look for the dog again. Just in case.

● ● ●

"I'll see your five and raise you ten more." Sally May Henderson tossed three red chips onto the pile in the middle of the table.

Eileen Callahan slapped her cards face down beside her. "I'm out."

Dorothy Wilson, grandmother to Becky Wilson from the veterinary clinic, tossed in a blue and a red chip. "See you."

"Too rich for my blood," Nora Brown added.

Carrying a huge tray over her left shoulder, Abbie Kane slowed by the table for the Saturday-morning poker game. "Do you ladies need a refill on those drinks?"

A chorus of "I'm good" sounded, except Eileen, who pointed with her chin to her near-empty glass. "I'll have another tea. Thanks."

"One sweet tea coming up." The words had barely escaped Abbie's lips when every head in the Silver Spurs Café turned to the front a full ten seconds before the old-fashioned bell announced the latest patron. And not any old ordinary patron. The woman Adam Farraday had driven into town at the crack of dawn.

Sally May pulled her cards close to her chest and shrugged. "Doesn't look like a hooker to me."

"Shh," three voices hushed, but it was Eileen's elbow that jabbed Sally May in the ribs. Lips pressed tightly shut, Eileen shot her friend of nearly thirty years a pointed glare.

Nora Brown, the youngest of the Tuckers Bluff Ladies Afternoon Social Club and a registered nurse at Eileen's nephew Brooks' medical practice—leaned in closer. "Didn't I hear Adam dropped her off at Ned's?"

"Yeah." Eileen nodded.

"Then it would make sense her car broke down, and Adam did the neighborly thing and gave her a ride into town."

Dorothy Wilson folded her cards in her hands. "And your point?"

"Why would anyone even jokingly suggest the woman was— you know—a professional? I mean, seriously, how blind do you have to be to think any of the Farraday men have to pay for company?"

"Thank you." A satisfied smile settled on Eileen's face. She'd moved in with her brother-in-law shortly after her sister Helen had died from giving birth to their only daughter, Grace. A mother bear couldn't be more protective of her cubs than Eileen was of her clan.

"Now don't get your knickers in a twist." Sally May spread

her cards on the table—two pairs, aces high. "You know I was only making fun of Burt Larson's comment that she was pretty enough to be one of them high-priced ladies of the night. We all know—even if your boys weren't good-looking enough to charm the panties off a nun—they were raised better than to be looking for that kind of company."

"Burt should stick to selling hammers and keep his thoughts to himself." Dorothy Wilson sprouted a grin as wide as Main Street. "And speaking of ladies." Laying three queens face up, she reached over and scooped the kitty toward her.

Nora gathered the cards together and shuffled. "The way you're grinning, Dorothy, you'd think we were playing with real money."

Sally swirled a chip between her fingers, her gaze on the pretty woman now sitting in a booth across the café. "I can see what Burt meant."

Nora squinted to get a better look across the room; Eileen rolled her eyes, and Dorothy asked, "How would you know?"

Sally cut the deck for Nora. "Not the call-girl part. The high-priced part. Her shoulders are so straight she looks like she's against a board. I bet, if you put a book on her head, it wouldn't fall off when she walks. And those clothes look more Neiman's than Walmart."

This time Eileen turned her head to look. "She's wearing pants and a shirt. What's not Walmart about that?"

As Nora dealt, everyone tossed a white chip on the table.

"You've been living with blue-jean-clad men too long. That's not just a shirt. It's buttoned-down, tailored and pressed. So are her pants. I didn't see her shoes, but I wouldn't be surprised if they're leather and a good name brand."

Dorothy examined her hand. "And this all matters why?"

"It doesn't." Eileen separated her cards, tossed down two and waited for Nora to deal her replacements. "Sally May is just happy to have something new to jaw about besides Ruth Ann's bunion surgery."

"Maybe." Sally dragged her attention from the attractive redhead and back to her own cards. "And maybe not."

"Still"—Dorothy sorted her cards—"does make a person wonder. What would bring a pretty big-city girl like that into this part of the country in the middle of the night?"

CHAPTER THREE

taring at the menu before her, Meg didn't have to look around to know all eyes in the place were still on her. She could feel the curious stares bouncing off her back. Not a surprise for a small town but damned uncomfortable nonetheless.

"Don't let them bother you." The waitress stood beside her, pad in hand.

"Excuse me?"

"Strangers don't come through here very often. It's like a highway pileup. They can't help but look."

Meg chuckled. "I've been called a lot of things but never a traffic wreck."

"No offense intended. So, have you decided what you want?"

A new life. But with only $22.84 in her wallet, Meg blew out a frustrated breath. Right about now a soothing bowl of Chef Andre's crab bisque soup would hit the spot nicely. "Just coffee please."

Abbie, according to her name tag, lifted a single scrutinizing brow before nodding. "One cup of coffee coming up."

What Meg wouldn't give to have her sensible sedan and her boring old life back. What a fool. Like an avalanche, she'd fallen hard and fast for Jonathan's good looks and charming ways. With a stellar diamond ring on her finger and wedded bliss around the corner, she'd mingled their bank accounts and credit cards. And, if that wasn't dumb enough, so delighted to have someone else in charge of the day-to-day tedium of finances and bill-paying, she'd gladly given the job to Jonathan without so much as a glance over his shoulder. Stupid, stupid, stupid. When had she become so blasted gullible? Whoever said love was blind wasn't kidding.

"Don't be so hard on yourself." Abbie slid a cup of coffee and a blueberry muffin in front of her. "Muffin's on the house. And here's another napkin."

Meg followed Abbie's gaze to her own hands and the paper napkin she'd turned and anxiously twisted into tatters.

"You got any experience waiting tables?"

"Excuse me?"

"My morning waitress just went on bed rest for the remainder of her pregnancy. If you're any good, there's an apron on a hook in the kitchen. You can start as soon as you finish that coffee." She offered a half smile, her eyes twinkling with amusement. "Even if you're not any good, you can still step in for Donna. Folks around here can forgive a pretty girl almost anything."

"I—"

"You think on it while you work on that muffin."

Before Meg could form a thought, never mind a response, the woman—who was clearly more than just an employee—had moved to the table where four women sat, playing cards.

Could Meg do the job? Did eating out on a regular basis automatically qualify her to wait tables? Her position at the hotel didn't include overseeing the restaurant. Oh, for heaven's sake, how hard could it be? Take an order. Give it to the chef—or cook. Carry it back to the table. Any idiot could do it. And she was no idiot. Normally.

She did need some place to lay low, and sort through the reality of what her life had become and just how much trouble trusting Jonathan had left her in. And then there was her father. For now it was best if even he didn't know where she was. Besides, without a car, she wasn't going anywhere else anytime soon. If only she hadn't left the ring in the hotel safe rather than wear it for the ceremony, she might have been able to use that as collateral for the new radiator. Waiting tables might at least pay for a place to stay until she could afford the repairs.

A tiny sledge hammer banged a rhythmic tattoo between her temples. What other choice did she have?

● ● ●

"Margaret Colleen O'Brien. You're sure?" Juggling the phone on his shoulder, Adam scribbled the name on a scratch pad in front of him.

"The town doesn't pay me to get something as simple as running a license plate wrong. New model Ferrari 458 Italia with vanity plates IM HIS is registered to Ms. O'Brien out of Dallas. Now will you tell me what this is all about?"

Leaning back in his chair, Adam propped up his feet and hoped the relaxed pose would reflect in his voice. "I told you. Stranger broke down outside of town. Thought the car might be stolen. Didn't want Ned getting in over his head."

"Right. Ned."

Adam could see the wheels turning in his little brother's head. Well, not so little any more. All the Farraday men were chips off the old block. Also standing six four, D.J.'s chip wasn't much different from Adam's.

"Tell me," his brother continued, "does this Margaret Colleen O'Brien have anything to do with the Meg O'Brien who Abbie just hired on at the Silver Spurs?"

"What?" His booted feet fell from their perch with a loud *thunk*.

"Abbie just hired a Meg O'Brien to fill in for Donna while she's on bed rest."

"You're sure?"

"If you keep asking me that, I won't be so nice the next time you need a favor."

"Never mind. I hear my next patient." Not wanting to know what D.J. was about to say next, Adam dropped the phone in its cradle and glanced out the window to the café across the street. What was his angel-in-white's story? Why did she lie about the car not being hers? And what the hell was she doing working at the Silver Spurs?

"Mrs Peabody called in. She's canceling her one o'clock to

see why Sadie's been off her food. And I quote, 'The little hussy just popped out two kittens on my favorite sweater.'" Becky laughed, then swallowed her grin. "Shall we lock the doors and grab a real lunch break? I heard Abbie has hired a replacement for Donna. I've been dying to find a minute to go check her out. If I go over there alone, Gran will snag me into their weekly poker game."

Adam pushed away from his desk. "Did the calico get picked up already?"

Becky nodded. "An hour ago. Shadow, the black Lab, is lifting his head. Pat's keeping an eye on him. No one is due in for an hour and a half. And we'll just be across the street if an emergency comes in."

"In that case"—he grabbed his hat off the hook, tipped it at her—"would you do me the honor, Miss Wilson, of joining me for lunch?"

"Why, kind sir"—she batted her lashes—"I'd be delighted."

Normally Adam didn't take a lunch break. If he ate at all, it was while sorting through paperwork at his desk or running between patients. The days he made farm and ranch calls for the bigger animals, a bag of chips often substituted for lunch. On a typical clinic morning he'd have a few scheduled patients. A cat to be spayed. A wellness visit for the family dog. A lethargic pet rabbit that, like Mrs. Peabody's cat, turned out not to be sick at all but pregnant. But the surprises and emergency surgeries were what kept him in constant motion, and often working late. The dog hit by the car protecting his favorite boy. Or the one that swallowed broken glass or a chicken bone.

Adding to the chaos were his emergency runs to nearby ranches. The prized mare in trouble foaling. Or a cow who somehow tangled herself in the barbed wire fencing. Other than finding a runaway bride broken down on a nearly deserted road, today had been the most uneventful day in a very long while.

Stopping at the front desk, he lightly tapped his college ring on the counter. Kelly, his receptionist, lifted her gaze from the stack of papers in front of her. "Becky and I are going across the street for a quick lunch. Pat's got things covered in the back. Care to join us? It's on me."

Kelly's eyes darted from the front window to the stacks of papers and back. "Oh, I'd love to check out the new waitress, but I brought lunch, and this work won't get done by itself."

"If you change your mind, you know where to find us."

Outside, a calm sixty-degree day passed under sunny skies. Spring weather had blown in early. Perfect for saddling a horse and riding to the creek for a cool dip. As kids, when their chores were done, he and his brothers could spend hours splashing and cooling off. On a slow day like today, driving out to the ranch and talking his brother Finn into playing hooky and going fishing seemed almost obligatory.

At the threshold of the café, Adam held the door open for Becky. The rest of the world might be modern and independent, but, in Tuckers Bluff, chivalry was still at least partly alive.

"Table for two, or are Pat and Kelly coming along?" Abbie asked hurriedly.

Adam removed his hat and held up two fingers. "Just us today."

"All I've got left is the booth in the back. If I'd have known hiring on a stranger would be such a boon for business, I'd have done this years ago." Abbie pointed her thumb over her shoulder. "Go on ahead and seat yourselves. I'll send Meg your way."

From his seat in the back, Adam had a bird's-eye view of the comings and goings of the only restaurant in town. Abbie shuffled quickly from table to table, offering just enough smile and conversation to fulfill her small-town duty, but Adam saw no sign of the stranded bride.

"Shouldn't you go say hi to your grandmother?" he asked, casually scanning the place for the new waitress.

"I'll pop over after we've ordered. This way, once the food's cooking, I'll have an excuse not to get roped into joining them."

"Don't like poker?"

"Oh, I love playing cards. Any cards. But, with that bunch,

there's no such thing as one quick hand, and, as it happens, I have a great job with a very cool boss that I'd rather not lose."

"Never happen. I have an in with that very cool boss, and the word is, he doesn't want to lose you either."

From the corner of his eye he saw the redhead hurrying toward their table with two glasses of water. She'd shed her bridal attire and wore one of the café's aprons over a button-down shirt and a dark pair of pants that stopped just below her knees, showing off shapely calves. His mind drifted back to his brief view of her ample cleavage on the road this morning, and he felt an unexpected jolt of electricity south of his belt buckle.

"Here you go." Meg smiled at Becky as she set down the water, then recognized Adam. "Oh, hi."

"Hi. I'm sorry I had to run out on you, but I was late for my early morning date with a golden retriever."

"Don't give it another thought." Meg waved him off with a smile. "Ned explained. I'm just glad you happened along when you did."

Before he could say another word, the order-up bell dinged and, raising a finger in the air, she mumbled, "I'll be right back," and took off toward the kitchen.

"Does she look a bit nervous to you?" Becky spoke to him, but her gaze remained on Meg, now standing behind the counter, holding a dish in one hand and studying a small piece of paper with the other.

"If I were a betting man, I'd say she hasn't done this before."

He couldn't hear what Meg and the cook were saying, but Abbie had moved in beside Meg, taken the slip of paper from Meg's hand, skewered it onto a nearby spike and handed Meg another plate of food.

After delivering it to the poker ladies, Meg trotted back to their table. "So, what will it be?"

Abbie kept the day's specials on the blackboard behind the counter. All the locals knew the menu by heart, so the fact no one had given them a menu had little impact. Only, at the same moment Adam was about to open his mouth to order, Meg apparently realized they were missing menus, and once again she did the finger-in-the-air thing, while she mumbled, "Be right back."

"Oh, yeah." Becky chuckled under her breath. "Definitely never done this before."

And not for the first time today, Adam found himself wondering—what was Margaret Colleen O'Brien's story?

CHAPTER FOUR

At least Meg had made enough in tips to pay for a couple nights in a cheap motel. Assuming there was a cheap motel in this town. The café had been nonstop busy all day. She'd barely had time to glimpse out the window at the few nearby stores and the animal clinic across the street.

And the veterinarian across the street.

In the dim light of daybreak the guy had looked pretty damn handsome. But, at that hour, *handsome* was often dependent on the lack of light. By midday, reality often came crashing down. But reality agreed with Adam Farraday. A whole lot.

Sexy cowboys on the covers of romance novels had nothing on him. Except for the brilliant color to his Irish blue eyes, his near-ebony hair and tanned skin brought new visuals to the words tall, dark and handsome.

Abbie sat beside Meg, hooking her foot around the nearest chair. Abbie pulled it close enough to rest her feet on. "Honey, you are definitely good for business."

"I didn't think it would be so hard."

"You did just fine for a greenhorn."

"I will never complain about table service again as long as I live." Everywhere she'd ever eaten had made waitressing seem so easy. Take an order, pass it on, then serve it. Who knew you needed a computerized brain to remember which meals came with salad and which didn't, which item on the menu was complete and which ones you had to remember to ask what sides they wanted? Never mind remembering all the side options, and, for a small café, Abbie had one heck of a long list of sides. And, if that wasn't enough for Meg's tired brain to tackle, the specials for the day had to be memorized, including how they're cooked. And, on top of all that, she had to know the ingredients as well. She hadn't a clue how many people had different food allergies. Nope, she would never complain about wait staff service ever again.

Abbie's attention flickered to the door. A policeman came through, and Meg sucked in a steadying breath. He tipped his Stetson, and then he took a seat at the counter. Abbie kept an eye on the good-looking patron, bantering with the afternoon waitress until Shannon poured him a cup of coffee and moved on, pot in hand, to the few occupied tables. Not until the officer nodded a silent greeting to both Abbie and Meg, and then took a slow sip of the hot brew, did Meg breathe easy again.

Her new employer's gaze swung back to Meg. "You'll have to pick up your bags from Ned's."

That would be *bag*. As in one. And all that contained was her makeup kit since she now wore the clothes she'd changed out of before arriving at the church. Her bags for the honeymoon—filled with all new clothes—were already at the hotel suite where they'd have stayed until this morning's flight. Sadly what she could afford tonight for her aching feet wouldn't be anything close to the lush honeymoon suite at the Belmont. "Where's the closest motel?"

"Butler Springs," Abbie mumbled, her gaze darting back to Shannon at another table. Abbie's lips curved slightly, watching the easy way Shannon handled her customers.

Considering Meg had made enough mistakes—forgotten enough menus, orders, drinks and entire tables to fill the Dallas Cowboys' Stadium—it was a miracle Abbie hadn't thrown her out on her ass yet. "That's not the name of a street around the corner, is it?"

Still smiling, Abbie returned her attention to Meg and shook her head. "Ninety miles north of here."

Terrific. Now what? She certainly couldn't walk ninety miles to and from work. Especially not the way her feet felt. Anne Klein made fabulous footwear but not for eight-hour shifts on her feet. "Bed-and-breakfast?"

Another twist of Abbie's head went to and fro. "Myrtle Yantz used to rent out a few rooms after her husband died, but she locked up the house and moved to Lubbock to be closer to her new grandbaby."

Chalk up one more reason to castrate Jonathan Cox if Meg ever saw him again.

"The original owner of the café lived in the apartment upstairs. We use it mostly for storage, but I keep one room for sleeping during an occasional emergency when I can't go home." Abbie reached into her pocket and pulled out a single key on a cowboy boot key chain. "There's probably a foot of dust up there, but it's all yours."

The way she felt, sleeping on a foot of dust would be just fine. "Thank you." After a long hot shower and a good night's sleep, she'd be better prepared to figure out what to do next. Pushing to her feet, Meg took in a deep breath and looked around.

"If you go straight through the kitchen to the back hall, the stairs are to your right. There's another entrance outside around the corner." Abbie dropped her feet to the floor and slid from the booth. "I'd better refill the ketchup bottles before the supper crowd starts trickling in. No telling how many people will show up, thinking you're still here."

"I can stay and help with that."

Setting her hand on Meg's arm, Abbie offered a bright smile. "You've done enough for your first day. Go on and settle in. I'll see you tomorrow morning for breakfast, but your first shift will be Monday. We start at 6:00 a.m."

"Six o'clock," Meg repeated on her way out the front door, silently debating if she'd lost her mind. As much as her feet screamed for relief, checking out her new home would have to take a backseat to doing a little shopping. A quick glance down the block told her downtown Tuckers Bluff might be able to provide her with a few basic necessities to get her through the next couple of days. Turning to her right she started down the street, taking in the different shops as she passed. The window for Haddie's Haven displayed a rainbow of yarn and fabric.

She passed Fred's Hardware, the Cut and Curl, Secondhand Rose gently used furniture store and stopped in front of a little shop called Sisters. What she needed was a Walmart, but the picturesque Main Street was all she had at her disposal. Opening the door to Sisters, she stepped inside.

"Welcome." A tall, thin strawberry redhead in jeans and a plaid shirt set the magazine in her hand on the counter and slipped a pencil behind her ear. "You must be the talk of the town. I'm Sissy."

"Oh, I thought I heard the bell." From behind a floral curtain a plump woman—no taller than Meg's chin— with platinum blonde hair teased into a 1950s' style beehive—practically glided across the room.

"How can Sister and I help you?" the redhead asked.

Sisters? Meg hoped her surprise didn't show. Obviously the women favored two different parents. "I need a few things. A couple of shirts and some new ... undergarments."

"I'm sure we have just what you need." Sissy curled her finger at Meg for her to follow. "Sister," Sissy said over her shoulder, "I'll show our guest the new cottons we received earlier this week. Why don't you go ahead and pull out some of our prettier lingerie?"

"Oh, yes, Sissy. Excellent idea." The woman waddled away, still talking. "Yes, we have some lovely things that will be perfect for our newest citizen."

Too tired to find her words, Meg wasn't about to correct the lady. Meg would only be here until ... how long would she be here? Almost stumbling to a stop, she shook her mind clear of questions she had no answer for and followed Sissy toward the back of the not-so-tiny shop. From the outside the place looked to be a quaint boutique, but now Meg could see it was the town's version of a department store. She walked past the children's section, a meager array of shoes, one rack of shirts and another of pants that passed for a men's department, and held back a smile. Maybe because she'd been on her feet all day or maybe because she'd never been in such a small town before, but an image of some of the good old boys she'd served at the café today coming here to buy clothes from Sissy and Sister gave Meg the first real laugh she'd had in days.

"Here we are." Sissy held up two blouses. Simple, lovely, very much Meg's style. The words "I'll take them" were on the tip of her tongue when she remembered she couldn't use credit cards—not until she figured out the best thing to do—and had little cash. Taking one hanger from Sissy, Meg lifted the blouse and, with her other hand, fingered the collar, slid down over the buttons and did her best to casually eye the price tag.

"We're running an introductory sale," Sissy said with a smile.

Even if Sister's eyes hadn't rounded like a pair of ping-pong balls, Meg had spent enough time shopping to know sales always came at the end of a season, not the beginning. Was there anyone in town who didn't intuitively know she was nearly penniless and alone?

"Two for one," Sissy added at Meg's silence, then, passing her the other shirt, took a tray of panties from her sister. "And these should do you well. Sister has an excellent eye for size."

The two button-down blouses in one hand, Meg lifted a single pair of cotton and lace panties with her other hand, carefully searching for prices. She still didn't know how much the blouses she held cost. Regardless of the sudden sale, affording more than a couple of pairs of underpants might not be easy, especially if she needed new shoes too.

Glancing at the two women, staring at her like a set of owl bookends, Meg had no choice. "How much are these?"

"We have layaway," the redhead said at the same time the plump sister announced, "Five dollars a pair or five for twenty dollars."

Once again the blonde with the beehive did a poor job of hiding her surprise.

Meg let the pretty panties fall back into the tray. "Maybe some plain cotton. And a pair of comfortable shoes." She could wash out her clothes and come shopping again on Monday with more tip money.

"Oh, yes." Sister set the tray of panties on the nearby glass counter that was clearly the jewelry department and bounced over to the shoes and held up a sensible black one. "These aren't very pretty, but they have wonderful arch support."

Arch support might very well be the two most beautiful words Meg had ever heard.

"Sister," Sissy said, "find her size and let her try them on."

Nodding, Meg handed Sissy the two blouses, walked over to the shoes and took a seat in the one straight-back chair. Right about now, as the two sisters cast furtive glances back and forth in silent communication, it occurred to Meg that maybe none of today had really happened. Maybe she was having some ridiculous wedding-jitters-induced nightmare. Nowhere in the real world were two women named Sister and Sissy, nor did a restaurant owner hire an incompetent waitress, nor did a tall, dark and handsome stranger come to the rescue at the crack of dawn like a knight in shining armor. The only thing required for the whole thing to be cemented as a dream would have been for Adam Farraday to have ridden up on a stallion and for Sister or Sissy to give her these shoes for free.

Maybe, if she closed her eyes really tight and told herself to wake up, she'd be back in Dallas, her fiancé would still be the man of her dreams, and the last thing she'd have to worry about was her father and the FBI. *Wake up, Meg. Wake up*. Slowly she opened her eyes to find Sister frowning only inches away.

Holding up a pair of brown slacks similar to the ones the other waitress Shannon had been wearing, Sissy elbowed her chubby sibling. "We offer credit too."

• • •

Elbows on the desk, Adam pressed the heels of his palms against his brows. On a dime, the quiet morning had turned into a chaotic afternoon. Bone tired didn't even begin to describe the way he felt.

"Should I put on another pot of coffee?" Becky asked from the doorway.

"No." Adam lifted his head and rolled his neck. "I need to call it a day."

"More like a night." With her nose, Becky pointed to the clock on the opposite wall. Almost seven.

He should have left an hour ago. "Why are you still here?"

Blowing out a sigh, Becky crossed her arms and shot him an *are you really that daft* glare.

Adam bit back a smile. Some days he felt like he was the one twelve years Becky's junior. "You're way too young to remind me of your grandmother, and I'm too old for you to be watching out for me."

Letting out another sigh, she pushed away from the wall and shaking her head, eased across the office to his desk and held up the unopened yogurt she'd left for him before he'd gone into surgery. Instead of going home where he belonged to get some much-needed sleep, he'd done a last-minute lancing of an abscess on Mrs. Perkens' cat. "Could have fooled me."

"Okay. You win. Maybe an occasional looking after." Some days he wondered how such a wise and caring woman could be hidden inside such a sweet young person. Being one of his sister, Grace's, best friends, Adam had watched the girls grow up. Where Grace was free-spirited, often irresponsible and, much to everyone's chagrin, frequently reckless, Becky was traditional, responsible and more dependable than a Swiss watch.

Shrugging out of his lab coat and hanging it on the nearby hook, Adam turned to rest his free hand against the small of her back and nudged Becky toward the hall. "But no more tonight. You go home and fuss over your grandmother. Or, better yet, shouldn't you be out with Ben on a Saturday night?"

Walking ahead of him down the hall, Becky shrugged. "Nah. Ben's been keeping company with the new teacher."

"Man has no taste." Not that Adam knew a thing about the

new teacher, but any man who let a girl like Becky get away was a fool and a half. Then again, maybe the bigger fool was the man who didn't see her in the first place. If his younger brother Ethan didn't open his eyes and smarten up pretty soon, Adam might just have to smack some sense into him. A girl like Becky wouldn't wait around for him forever.

Becky reached for the front door as Adam scooted around her, holding it open. Shaking her head again, she said, "The man who spent his senior year of high school dating Emily Taub has no business criticizing anyone's taste."

"Emily was very pretty."

"And very plastic."

Both of them standing on the front porch, he turned to lock the door. He remembered many things about Emily Taub. Most he wasn't willing to bring up in mixed company, and none of them involved the word *plastic*.

By the time he'd spun about, Becky had already climbed into the front seat of her car. "See you Monday morning."

With a quick nod and short wave, she was on her way down the road. Adam looked across the street to the café. He doubted Meg O'Brien was still working. Though he hadn't heard otherwise, he doubted she was even still employed after her challenging performance today. Regardless, he'd get tonight's special to go. With any luck he'd be home, fed and down for the evening sooner than later.

The overhead bell rang at the Silver Spurs as he walked in the door. Not much of a crowd at this hour. Early to bed, early to rise was a rancher's creed. Most of the patrons scattered about were couples enjoying a Saturday night date. His brother D.J. sat at the counter in the corner, his back to the kitchen.

Abbie looked up from pouring coffee. "Evening special?"

Adam nodded.

"My favorite kind of customer. Eats whatever we cook. One meat loaf special coming up." She disappeared through the double kitchen doors.

"Quiet night?" Adam straddled the stool beside D.J.

"Shh." He raised his hand. "You'll jinx it."

Adam laughed. Out in the middle of Nowhere, Texas, the strangest damn things could happen. While a city cop's biggest fear was an active shooter call at shift end followed by mounds of paperwork or, worse, hours with the crime scene team, a country lawman had to be concerned with teens tipping cows and blowing up hollow logs for entertainment. Not that the growing Butler County didn't have its share of mostly petty criminal activity, but Tuckers Bluff was simply not the hub of felony country.

"Have a cup?" D.J. asked.

"No. The last thing I want now is caffeine." He slapped his palm face down on the counter. "I'm seriously considering taking forty winks right here while Abbie boxes up supper."

"Tough day, rescuing your damsel in distress and all."

That had been the easy part. Keeping his mind on his work and off said damsel had been another story. "Heard any word on how long she'll be staying in town?"

D.J. shrugged. "Don't think anyone knows."

"Here you go." Abbie set a white paper bag on the counter. "Added a little extra. You're looking a bit thin. Eileen won't forgive me if I let you start withering away."

If every cell in his body wasn't exhausted, he'd have laughed at the fear of God his aunt Eileen put in everyone. The woman should run for mayor. She and Dorothy Wilson. They'd make one hell of a team. Wouldn't need a town council. They could run the whole show by themselves.

"Consider it a little thank-you for the new boon to business," Abbie added.

"Excuse me?"

"Meg. My new waitress. The one you rescued this morning."

Adam was glad he was sitting down. He'd thought for sure Meg had been so far in over her head that her first day would have been her last. "She still works here?"

Abbie let out a cackle from deep in her belly. "Do I look

stupid? That woman has brought in a week's worth of business today. Besides"—her smile dimmed—"she's in a bad spot."

"She told you that?" On the drive into town, the wayward bride had barely said a word to him.

"Don't need to hear the words. Could see it in her eyes. She ordered coffee for lunch. I called ahead to the sisters. Figured she'd be coming in to get a more practical wardrobe for working here."

D.J. nodded his approval to the café owner. "That was nice of you, Abbie."

"Got nothing to do with nice. It's why none of us live in big cities anymore. People are worth giving a damn about." She whirled around, coffeepot in hand, and went about her business of keeping her patrons happy.

"She has a point." D.J. stared off in Abbie's direction.

"About being decent?"

"Not living in cities anymore."

Adam wasn't completely sure what happened to bring D.J. back to Tuckers Bluff. Some things even brothers didn't talk about. But Adam did know that his dad and Aunt Eileen were happiest when the Sunday supper table was full. Especially when Connor and Ethan made it home. "You coming to the ranch tomorrow?"

"Don't I always?" D.J. nodded. A slow, steady grin formed.

Pushing to his feet, Adam slapped his brother on the shoulder. "See ya then."

The distance from the café to his apartment was the mere width of the two-lane road and the sidewalk in front of the clinic, and yet, from where he stood, it might as well have been a football field away. Standing here, contemplating how tired he was, would not get him into bed any faster. Putting one foot in front of the other, he seriously considered saving the meat loaf for breakfast. Nothing seemed more appetizing now than his bed. So, of course, only one other thought sprang to mind. Where was Margaret Colleen O'Brien sleeping tonight?

CHAPTER FIVE

esides the hard work of the wait staff, there were two more things that Meg had underappreciated her entire life. A good mattress and hot water. Both of which had done wonders for all her aching body parts. Working out was a normal part of her daily routine. It had never occurred to her that she was in anything but good shape. She'd even done barre classes to stay flexible, but none of it compared to the hours on her feet yesterday, carrying dishes and taking orders. Every muscle, no matter how small, had screamed surrender.

From a quick survey when she'd arrived at her new digs last night, Meg had calculated that the original floor plan for the café apartment used only half the ground floor footprint. In the large living and dining area all sorts of boxes were piled atop each other and the furniture, filing cabinets were crammed in the space along with other bits and pieces. The kitchenette area had even more boxes stacked from countertop to ceiling. The only free spaces were the vintage bedroom with an old spring-style metal bed and the bathroom, which had a phenomenal claw-foot tub.

Despite Abbie's warning of a foot of dust, Meg had found both areas in pretty good shape. A linen closet stuffed full had a surprising amount of towels, sheets, tablecloths and napkins for an uninhabited apartment. It had taken her only a short while to put the cleaning supplies from the broom closet to good use. In the oversize bathroom, she'd discovered a full washer and dryer for the sheets and spent more time than she should have soaking in the old tub. Why anyone thought it was more practical, convenient or fashionable to install stubby tubs in contemporary houses, she had no idea. If she ever got her own home again, a big cast-iron soaker tub was going to be at the top on her list of wants. Right after an honest husband and peace of mind.

Scratch the husband. Men were highly overrated and most definitely more trouble than they were worth.

Putting on the single pair of slacks and the one top she'd bought in town—paying cash for everything to Sister's delight—Meg slipped on her own shoes and realized breakfast was only a flight of stairs away.

The smell of bacon and sausage grew stronger with every step. By the time she pushed through the unlocked door from the rear hall to the café kitchen, Meg's stomach was roaring like the engine of that blasted sports car.

"Good morning," Abbie said without looking up. "Coffee's on. Frank will make you anything you want. The hot plate upstairs doesn't work."

Under all the boxes and clutter, Meg hadn't even noticed a hot plate. "Thanks. Eggs and toast will be fine."

Abbie pointed to the bread and multiple-slice toaster at the opposite side of the kitchen. "Help yourself to anything you want. When you've got your food, come on out and have a seat in front, and we'll talk."

Meg's appetite took a fast dive. Her mind insisted she stay calm; her heartbeat believed otherwise. And her heart was probably right. Abbie had most likely reconsidered Meg's value and, after feeding her breakfast, would be giving her the proverbial pink slip. Her mouth went dry, and her throat closed. Yesterday she'd been too damn mad at her ex to be very afraid. In the light of day, her immediate future scared the hell out of her.

The food's-up bell rang, pulling Meg from her morbid thoughts. Frank had slipped her plate onto the pickup shelf. "Breakfast on deck."

"Thank you." She did her best to smile and screw up her courage. Taking the plate, she turned to deal with whatever Abbie had to say.

Across the café, looking down, Abbie sat in a back corner booth with a stack of papers on one side, a mug of coffee to her right and what looked like a ledger book in front of her. "Take a load off. You'll be on your feet enough tomorrow. Remember we open at six. Donna usually has the breakfast shift so you'll fill in for her. You'll work past lunch. Shannon comes in around two. If there's a problem ..." Abbie looked up and frowned. "Close your mouth. You'll catch flies."

Meg's mouth snapped shut so fast she heard her teeth clack. "Excuse me?"

"Your face. You look like I just told you that you'll be running a full marathon butt naked in winter. Is breakfast and lunch too much work for you?"

"No. No. Not at all." At least she hoped not.

"Then what?" Abbie leaned back, took a sip of coffee.

"I ... I thought I was fired."

Setting her cup down hard, the hot liquid sloshed over the top. Abbie laughed until she began coughing. "Fire you? Honey, you're my rainy day fund. Oh, I know the *new* will wear off soon, and things will get back to normal, but it's not often this place does more than break even. I'm taking full advantage for as long as it lasts. Now are you up to handling the breakfast and lunch shifts?"

Meg bobbed her head up and down, and her stomach rumbled with hunger and delight. She never would have thought she could be so happy to have a job waiting tables, but this morning it felt like the best damn job in the world.

The phone beside yesterday's receipts buzzed against the table. Abbie grabbed it with one hand and waved at Meg to start eating with the other. "Hello. ... Hi, Miss Eileen. ... Yes, that's right. ... Yes, yes, she is. One minute." Abbie held out the phone. "It's for you."

If Meg looked startled before, she no doubt looked stunned now. Could her father have found her already? No. ... Abbie had said *Miss Eileen*. Meg took the cell and slowly raised it to her ear. "Hello?"

"Good morning," a woman said with a strong voice. "I'm Eileen Callahan. You met my nephew Adam yesterday morning."

"Yes, ma'am. He was very helpful. Thank you."

"I'm glad to hear that. I know you're new in town, and it's not easy getting settled in."

Meg almost laughed. Not much to settle in with only the clothes on your back. "Abbie is making settling in easy."

"Good. Glad to hear it. In these parts Sunday is family day," Eileen continued. "I look forward to having you over for supper."

"Oh, well, thank you. I'm sure that would be lovely sometime soon, but—"

"I know your car is in Ned's garage so you'll be needing a ride."

Meg felt sure two different conversations were going on here. "Well, once Ned gets the new radiator in, it won't take that long to—"

"Yes, I heard about the long wait for parts. So sorry about that. A good family meal is just the ticket to forget about life's irritations."

"Normally I'd agree with you, but—"

"Good. Adam has business at the Thomas ranch so Brooks will be picking you up."

"Oh." Meg swallowed hard. She was not ready to play nice with the neighbors. Playing nice usually led to questions, and she was far from ready to answer any. "I didn't mean—"

"He'll be by for you at two."

"But I don't—"

"Is that too early? Will two thirty be better for you?"

The lady sounded so damn nice and determined. "Uh, no. Two will be fine. Thank you."

"Wonderful. See you soon." The call disconnected, and Meg returned the phone to her new boss.

"Let me guess." Abbie grinned. "D.J.'s picking you up for Sunday supper."

Meg shook her head. "Brooks."

"Good choice." Abbie smiled.

"Mm." Meg wondered what business did she have at a

Farraday family dinner. She wasn't family. To everyone except Adam, who apparently would not be there, she was a perfect stranger. "How did that happen?"

"Eileen Callahan happened, that's how." Abbie leaned forward and patted Meg's hand. "I know you're used to city ways, but things are done a little differently out here. Neighborly is more than semantics. Think of Miss Eileen as the matriarch of Tuckers Bluff and the head of the welcoming committee. If you'd moved into a local home, by now you'd have a freezer full of blueberry muffins and King Ranch casseroles."

Despite the nerves wrangling in her stomach, Meg felt the hints of a real smile on her lips. "If the casseroles are as good as the fried version at the fair, it might be worth finding a house of my own."

"A sense of humor. Good. Glad to have you here, Meg O'Brien. Now I'll need you to fill out this form." Abbie pushed a W-4 across the table and leveled her gaze on Meg's.

If she filled this out, if her employment was reported, they'd find her. She couldn't look Abbie in the eyes. Now what?

"Meg"—Abbie covered her hand again—"is someone after you? You don't have to be afraid."

"What?" Meg lifted her gaze from the paper. Deep concern, leaning toward fear, stared back at her. All of Abbie's help suddenly made sense. She must think Meg was running from an abusive relationship. "No. Nothing like that." Meg wasn't the one in trouble exactly.

Abbie leaned back and dipped her chin in a curt motion of acceptance. "This goes into a folder in my filing cabinet. The IRS won't know you're here until I send out W-2s in January."

Meg didn't say a word. She pulled the paper in closer, accepted the pen Abbie held and signed the form. "Thank you."

• • •

"Just this once, can we start with dessert?" Adam dropped his hat on the nearby rack, and followed his nose to the kitchen and his aunt Eileen's homemade blueberry pie. "I'll eat mine now."

With her back to him, Eileen turned, a dishrag in each hand, holding a warm pie. "The rules have been the same for twenty-five years. They're not changing today." Her voice was stern, but her eyes twinkled with humor.

"Get in line, bro." D.J. came in the back door and lifted his nose in his aunt's direction. "I could smell those delicious pies halfway to the house."

Sneaking up behind his aunt as she set the pie on the cooling rack, Adam looped his arms around her waist, kissed her cheek and whispered in her ear, "Admit it. The pie is for your favorite. Me."

Batting away his hands, she spun in place. "I have no favorites, Adam Farraday, and you know it." Then she pushed on tiptoe and, with her hand on his jaw, gave him a peck on the cheek.

"How's the new calf doing?" Adam opened the fridge and grabbed a couple of Shiner Bocks, tossing one to his brother.

"That is not a football." Eileen huffed, hands on hips. "Can't you just hand your brother a beer? Do you have to throw it?"

"That would mean they'd have to give up their adolescent shenanigans." Finnegan "Finn" Farraday, the second youngest of the clan—the one whose blood ran ranch-house red and the one who rode roughshod over his siblings as if he were the firstborn—brushed his boots clean by the back door. "We'll just have to accept that these two yahoos are never going to grow up."

D.J. took a long swig, then pointed his longneck at his big brother. "I think the residents of Tuckers Bluff would take offense at referring to their chief of police as a *yahoo*."

"Why?" Finn took a beer for himself from the fridge. "I didn't call *them* yahoos."

The back door swung open again and then shut with a thud. Over six foot himself, and still as strong and sturdy as any of his sons, Sean Patrick Farraday headed for the kitchen sink and turned on the faucets. "There's a line of fence down by Brennan's barn. I rigged it for now, but we'll have to do it right in the morning."

D.J. reached for a bag of chips off the top of the fridge. "I think it's time we stopped patching his old fence and just replaced that section. I'm not sure what's older, him or those rickety posts. When a strong wind is enough to knock over an entire section of fence, it's time to build a new one."

A stony glare from aunt Eileen had D.J. putting the chips back, obeying the same way they all had when they were kids. By the time they were teens, every one of the boys could read her looks. This particular one clearly shouted DO NOT SPOIL YOUR SUPPER.

"We can't replace it without his permission. And the man's too stubborn to accept a little neighborly elbow grease." Adam took his regular place at the kitchen table. "So how is the calf?"

"Fine." Finn eyed the warm pies. "Have to keep bottle-feeding him though."

"What's keeping Brooks?" Their dad helped himself to a tall glass of milk. Ever since he'd been diagnosed with a duodenal ulcer, he'd given up on beer and taken to drinking the soothing white liquid as though he were a growing calf.

"He had to make a stop." Eileen set a stack of dishes on the kitchen table. "We're having company. One of you boys set the dining room table."

All four Farraday men turned to stare at her.

"Don't look at me like that. Someone get the silverware. The good stuff."

Stunned at having Sunday supper in a room reserved for Christmas, Thanksgiving and the occasional wake, Adam and his brothers stood rooted to the floor. A second later their father gave them the other half of the *do as you're told* glare that he and their aunt had perfected so long ago.

The only one to have done any serious work this morning, Finn was automatically excused from last-minute chores while he ran upstairs to wash up. D.J. was already by the buffet, counting out the good silver. The patriarch of the Farraday brood spread the tablecloth over the smooth mahogany table that had been in the family for generations. Carefully juggling the stack of dishes, Adam eased them onto the table. Though curiosity burned in everyone's eyes, no one was willing to ask the obvious. Who the hell was coming to supper?

CHAPTER SIX

"You, D.J., Finn, Adam, Connor, Ethan, and Grace." Meg kept a mental tally as she repeated each name. "Seven."

Brooks chuckled from the driver's seat of his Suburban. "At last count."

Earlier this afternoon she'd been sitting on the stool farthest away from the front door of the café, sipping a hot cup of tea, and watching the comings and goings of the patrons. The midafternoon interactions had been interesting. Yesterday—when she'd been rushing like a chicken with her head cut off, waiting on customers—she'd noticed very little about them. Remembered even less. Now she was able to see the way Abbie worked the room. On Sunday afternoons she was the only wait staff. Something about Sundays being for families, though she did a decent lunch crowd. Mostly folks coming in after church, Abbie had explained.

It was nice to see families arriving in their Sunday best. Little girls in pretty dresses and sons in their button-down shirts and slicked-back hair. A few teens took over the far corner where yesterday the ladies had been playing poker. A couple of the folks who'd come in alone sat at the counter. Burt Larson, the owner of Fred's Hardware store, had sat down beside her to chat a bit. A friendly old bachelor who had bought the business from Fred and hadn't seen any reason to change a name folks were used to, he seemed to know something about everyone in the diner and didn't mind sharing his knowledge. He also liked his hot tea with real cream. A little odd but something she'd remember for the next time he came in. Meg had noticed early on that Abbie knew every person not only by name but by their preferred drink as well.

"Will that be your usual diet cola, Miss Susan?"

"We're out of decaf, Harry. I've put a fresh pot on for you."

"Water, no ice, with a twist coming right up, Miss Cassie."

And everyone seemed to genuinely like Abbie. Not that there was anything about her not to like, but the feel was different here. Almost perfect. Like scenes from a black-and-white movie. The kind of film where small towns held square dances and barn-raising picnics. Unlike her world that relied on the bar scene and Internet dating to socialize, or insurance companies and TV attorneys to deal with property loss.

At exactly two o'clock on the nose, the bell at the café door dinged, and at first Meg thought Adam had come to get her after all. It took a few seconds to recognize the man at the door wasn't Adam, just a close double. Well over six foot, with broad shoulders, wearing the requisite west Texas jeans and well-worn boots, he had the same jet-black locks that Adam did, but, as he moved in her direction, it wasn't crystal blue eyes that spotted her. This man's eyes shone almost shamrock green. Eileen hadn't mentioned who Brooks was, but it was clear to anyone who could see that Adam and this man were brothers. Maybe even twins.

For the short ride from town he'd been filling her in on the rest of the family. It was much easier to keep him talking than answering the standard questions of where she came from and what was she doing in Tuckers Bluff.

"And you're a doctor."

He nodded.

"But, of the seven, only a few will be at dinner?" she asked. To an only child whose friends rarely had more than one or two siblings, keeping up with seven seemed like the making of a reality TV show.

"Finn, the youngest brother, he runs the ranch. He'll be there. Of course me, Adam, you've met. D.J.—"

"That's Declan James?"

"Correct." He nodded, turning onto a dirt road under a huge iron arch with a scrolling *F* dead center.

Bumping along, she was thankful to be in his large SUV and not her four-door sedan. Or worse, Jonathan's stupid sports car. West Texas had a thing or two to learn about paved streets.

"We're missing Ethan, Connor and Grace," Brooks finished.

Meg closed her eyes, running their names through her mind again, trying to remember who was who and who would she be meeting. Adam, Brooks, Connor, D.J. Her eyes flew open. "You're all in alphabetical order," she squealed.

A hearty laugh filled the space around her. "Took you a bit to catch on to that. Yes. Mom loved *Seven Brides for Seven Brothers*. Dad finally relented to naming us after the alphabet, but he refused to let her name us after the characters in the movie."

"But the oldest brother in the film was named Adam."

"Yes." Brooks steered around a bend in the road. "But Dad didn't figure out what she was up to until I was born. I was almost Benjamin. In the end they agreed on my grandmother Sarah's maiden name. Brookstone."

"I see." And she did. As soon as they came around the curve, a large home rose in the distance. Mostly natural wood. A cross between midcentury modern and log cabin, the structure stood proud in the midst of the surrounding yellow fields. "Wow."

Brooks smiled and slowed over the rocky drive.

Her eyes took in the details of the home as they drew closer. Flowers of all shades planted out front and hanging from assorted baskets on the porch. A massive porch with several rockers on either side of the front door. A few evergreens graced the sides of the property. A few more live oaks stretched their knotted branches, creating an oasis of shade near the front and back of the house, but the rest of the area was nothing but wide open space. She might still be in the state of Texas, but she had most definitely landed in a foreign world.

● ● ●

The front door creaked when Brooks held it open, and every head in the room looked up. Adam had almost looked to the place setting before him when he caught a flash of red, and his head shot back up. Meg O'Brien stepped over the threshold, a tentative smile on her face.

"Hello, dear." Eileen crossed the floor of the expansive living area. "So glad to have you."

"Thank you." The woman looked like she'd walked into an arena of snorting bulls. Her gaze scanned the area, and Adam thought she took a step back in preparation for retreat.

"You know Adam." Eileen pointed to him from the front hall and gently steered her to the kitchen where his brothers and father were.

Like a mindless idiot, he was still waving long after she'd left his view. His mind lingering on the gentle smile, the timid gaze and the casual sway of her hips as she crossed into the kitchen. This Meg was in complete contrast to the feisty, downright fiery woman he'd rescued by the roadside, and he wondered too easily which would she be in bed.

"Quite the looker." Brooks had come up behind him.

"Is she?" Sometimes saying less was the easiest way to save face. Adam focused on putting out the last of the dishes and slamming the brakes on his runaway thoughts.

"Reminds me of a skittish filly. Nice enough but she's hiding something. On the ride from town she managed to evade the simplest of questions until the conversation circled strictly around our family. What's the story?"

"How should I know?"

"You found her."

"And?" Adam raised his gaze to meet his brother's.

"You drove her to town."

"You drove her here *from* town. Why would I know any more than you?"

Brooks looked past him toward the kitchen. "Ned says she's a runaway bride. Think she's got a husband looking for her?"

When he'd seen the smeared makeup from a long cry, Adam

had assumed she'd been left at the altar. Could he have had it backward, and there was an abandoned husband on the hunt? "I don't know."

"Rumor has it she's got money. Why do you think she's working for Abbie?"

Hiding from her new husband? That idea irked him. A lot.

Laughter growing louder filtered into the dining room. His father was putting on his best Irish accent and telling stories about his uncle George. Walking beside him, Meg was chuckling. Just as the rest of the family hit the living room, she flashed his father a bright smile, and Adam's gut clenched.

All through supper Adam, sitting beside Meg, did his best not to stare at her. At least not to get caught at it. He also made an extra effort not to spring across the table and put his brothers in a headlock when they'd forget themselves and stare. Not that he blamed them. She was beautiful.

Aunt Eileen held out the breadbasket to her. "Have another. Tell us, how long do you expect to be staying in Tuckers Bluff?"

Her gaze shifted down just long enough for his aunt to shoot him a tight-lipped glance before Meg raised her eyes again. "I don't know yet. At least long enough for my car to get fixed."

"I know it's hard on a family these days with everyone spread so far apart." Eileen's smile stayed in place, but a far-off look filled her eyes.

"He'll be back." Sean reached over and patted his sister-in-law's hand.

For a few seconds the table grew quiet. It had been standard operating procedure in the Farraday clan to focus on the day Ethan returned to the family and not what he did now. Though they were all proud as hell of him, a marine helicopter pilot, his uniform was decorated with so much fruit salad that it showed he was better than damn good at his job. It was easier on everyone's nerves if no one had to consider what he'd done to earn all those medals. Especially not with company at Sunday supper.

Adam reached for another of his aunt's homemade biscuits.

"Anyone hear from our baby sister lately?"

"Oh, yes." Aunt Eileen sprouted a smile. "She called this morning to confirm she will be coming home the weekend of Sandra Lynn's wedding. Weddings are always good for bringing family together."

As much as he didn't want to, there was no stopping himself from taking a quick peek at Meg's reaction to wedding talk. He wasn't sure if he was hoping to determine whether she'd been the dumper or the dumpee, or if he was just plain worried about her feelings. But whichever the case was a moot point, as her expression was cool and calm, and gave no indication she might have been even a little melancholy over the comment.

"I understand"—Meg smiled—"that Grace is in law school."

"Her last year," Sean announced with pride. "For what it's costing, she should graduate as a Supreme Court judge."

"Now, Sean." Eileen rolled her eyes.

"I just hope she can fix parking tickets," Brooks said before shoving his last bite of roast in his mouth.

"Parking tickets?" Sean grumbled. "Three years of one of the best law schools in Texas and you're thinking parking tickets?"

"No one is getting any parking tickets. Not around here," D.J. added.

Eileen shook her head, chuckling. "It's not like we have meters."

D.J. reached for the last biscuit. "Let's hope she's aspiring to handling wills and small claims 'cause there won't be much else for her to do here."

Collecting her plate and that of her brother-in-law's, Eileen pushed to her feet. "You boys stop looking for trouble where there is none. Everyone needs a lawyer every once in a while. This may be a small town but it's a big enough county for one more lawyer."

"Here. Let me help." Meg stood and reached for Adam's empty plate.

"Nonsense. You're a guest." Eileen turned to D.J. "Why don't you show Meg around outside. Show her the new calf."

"Sorry." D.J. flashed an apologetic smile before turning back to the phone in his hand. "I need to get back to the office."

Aunt Eileen's face crumpled instantly with concern. "Something wrong?"

Still focusing on the screen in his hand, D.J. shook his head. "Not sure." Coming to the end of the text, he slid the phone into his pocket, met his aunt's steely gaze and, reaching forward, brushed the frown from her brow with his thumb. "Nothing for you to worry about." He kissed the top of her head and turned to the rest of the room. "Sorry to eat and run."

The room remained silent for a few seconds as D.J. grabbed his hat and worked his way to the front door. It wasn't often he got called away from a family supper. This part of cattle country was pretty tranquil. There hadn't been much excitement since the Brady boys spray-painted *I heart U* on Amanda Rankin's father's prize bull. Most of the serious crimes tended to happen in the bigger cities. The county seat particularly. But nothing guaranteed that one day real trouble couldn't come to Tuckers Bluff.

"Have you ever been on a ranch before?" Sean was the first to turn his attention away from his son and to his guest.

"Can't say that I have."

"Then Eileen's right. You need to see the new additions to the barn." He looked to Adam. "Why don't you take her outside?"

"That won't be nec—"

"You go along with my son. It never gets old seeing Mother Nature's miracles. Just don't name them."

Meg's eyes rounded like a barn owl, and Adam almost laughed. Growing up on a ranch, he'd learned fast never to name the calves, and, from the look on her face, for a city girl, Meg had figured out why pretty quick.

"Come on." Adam reached over and pulled out her chair. His fingers brushed against her side as she shifted away from the table, and he sucked in a breath. If he'd been a smart man, he'd have passed off this chore to Brooks. Then again, when it came to women, no one had ever claimed he was smart.

CHAPTER SEVEN

The shock at the feel of Adam's fingers on her side was so startling, so charged, Meg had glanced down to see if she could blame the carpet for static electricity. Well-polished hardwood floors had gleamed back at her. No rug.

"Barn's down this path here."

For her a *path* would be concrete, maybe blacktop, at least some sort of cobblestone or pavers. Out here, *path* clearly had a different meaning. When she'd first arrived at the ranch, she'd noticed most of the surrounding lands had been drab and bland in color, only the area immediately circling the house had scattered sprigs of new green growth. Especially under the shade of the occasional tree on either side of the "path." Trampled dirt and pebbles that gave new grass little opportunity to sprout drew a line toward a massive structure not too far in the distance.

"We ride over twelve hundred head of cattle on nearly one hundred thousand acres."

A hundred thousand? "That sounds really big."

"Big is relative. You need a lot of land per head to run cattle in this part of the state. Finn's had his eye on our neighbor Ralph Brennan's property." Adam slid open the barn door and stepped aside to let her go inside first.

She noticed he gave her a wide berth and wondered if the jolt of static electricity in the house had affected him as much as it had unsettled her.

"Brennan's getting to the point where he can't take on the ranch work anymore. Dad and Finn bought out his herd and lease the land for grazing. Just today Dad and Finn had to repair some downed fence for him."

"That was nice of them."

"Neighbors look out for each other around here."

"Doesn't the man have family?"

Adam bobbed his head. "Daughter and granddaughter somewhere east. Haven't seen them in years. I doubt they'd want to take over. Brennan promised Dad ages ago, if he sells, we get first dibs, and now my brother Connor has had his eye on the place too."

"Connor? He's the marine helicopter pilot?"

"No. That's Ethan. Connor is working in oil."

"That's right." Meg nodded. "The oil rigs."

"Means to an end. He's always wanted to expand horse breeding on the ranch with his own quarter horse stock, but now I think—when he's got enough saved—he wants a place of his own. Our sister, Grace, used to do barrel racing when she was a teen. A good horse made all the difference. Training too."

"And Connor knows how to do that?"

"More than knows. The kid has always had almost a magic touch with horses." Adam led the way deeper into the barn.

From what she could tell, the building's interior resembled any number of barns or stables she'd seen on a variety of TV shows. A wide center aisle with stalls on either side. Halfway through the cavernous space, he casually pointed out the tack and feed rooms. She assumed the feed rooms held food. *Tack* was anyone's guess. Pausing, Adam reached into a clear container on a shelf and drew out a couple of tan chunks. "Here, put these in your pocket."

Doing as instructed, she took a closer look at the small tub. All she could make out was a carrot on the label. Before she could ask questions, Adam moved on. She hurried to keep up with his long strides. In this part of the barn the expanse between the stall doors appeared larger. "These stalls are bigger."

"They are." He nodded. "Each has a back door of sorts so no one has to circle the building to get in or out of the stall."

"Why only some?"

"Different purposes. We might use the space for a

convalescing horse. Or one that is having problems being bullied—"

"Really? Horses do that?"

Adam blew out a terse grunt. "Sometimes we have more in common with animals than we might like to admit." He opened a stall door and stepped inside. "In this case, we had an expectant mare. One of Connor's foundation stock. Gives us plenty of room for when the foal comes. Just in case. This here is Ginger."

The dazzling smile that took over Adam's face had her craning her neck to peer eagerly inside. "Oh my."

Not that Meg was any reliable judge of horseflesh, but the animal standing in the large space was breathtaking. A gleaming shade of dark copper, head held high, the horse stepped forward, her eyes widening with what Meg thought was fear or fury. Either way, the animal was still gorgeous.

"Easy girl." Adam moved to pat the horse's neck while speaking to Meg. "Stay slightly to her side so she can see you."

Meg nodded but decided staying put was the smarter course of action. Then her gaze fell on the tiny shadow behind Ginger, and Meg gleefully waved a finger at it. "Oh, look, a baby."

Adam chuckled. "That would be Saffron. She's a filly, a female. The male foals are colts."

From behind her mama, a tiny head peeked around, studying Meg.

"Hi, Saffron," Meg cooed.

Mama horse's ears twitched.

"She's good. I promise," Adam reassured Ginger, then turned to face Meg. "Now would be a good time to take the carrot treats from your pocket. Hold them out, your palm perfectly flat, and let her come to you."

Ginger didn't seem all too sure she wanted to shift from her stance of guarding her foal, but, stretching her neck, she must have made a decision because, the next thing Meg knew, the horse's lips were tickling her palm as she gobbled up the snack. "May I touch her?"

Adam nodded. "She likes it if you rub down the side of her neck. Just remember not to move too fast and to keep your hands where she can see them."

"Hi there, Mama." Meg ran her palm along what she thought must be the horse's jaw. "You and your baby are so pretty." Ginger dipped her head down, then pulled back up as though agreeing, causing Meg to laugh. "It's like she understands."

Still smiling, Adam leaned back against the door and crossed his ankles. "Don't let anyone tell you otherwise. She absolutely understands every word we've said."

The foal with long knotty legs crept out from behind her mother, curious yet still timid. Adam held out his hand, drawing the young horse to him. "Come here, little one."

"Are you going to give her a treat too?"

Adam shook his head. "She's not ready for that yet. Just a good scratch along her neck."

The sight of man and newborn beast was fascinating. The curiosity in the young life and the sparkle in Adam's eyes. "You love what you do." It wasn't a question really.

"I do." Adam ran his hand along the foal's side. "As far back as I can remember, I was always fascinated with the animals. But, unlike Connor—who thrived on the rush and thrill of the free mustangs—I was more concerned over the bird with the broken wing, the bunny who'd lost his mother or the litter of barn cats. My mother said my first word wasn't *Mama* or *Papa*. It was *poepee*."

"*Poepee*?"

"That would be *pony*."

Meg smiled.

"I must have been ten when a favorite horse had trouble foaling. My dad did all he could. The vet was stuck in a storm clear across the county. We managed to save the foal but lost the mother. That was the day I decided I wanted to be a veterinarian."

"And you never changed your mind?"

He shook his head. "Never looked back."

Meg couldn't stop herself from staring at Saffron, the tiny

version of her mother, nuzzling Adam's hand. "Your dad is right. This is just amazing."

"It is." He pulled away and stood near the stall door. "One more thing to show you."

Meg ran her hand down the side of Ginger's neck. "Thank you for sharing your baby with me."

Once again Adam pressed himself against the doorway, allowing her as much space as possible to pass. Across the way, he leaned against the wall, lifting his chin to a point inside the stall. "This little guy arrived this morning."

Meg's cheeks pulled with another broad smile. Inside the stall, like a contented cat, a young calf lay curled on a bed of hay. "Isn't that adorable?"

Adam didn't answer; he simply nodded.

And then she remembered what Mr. Farraday had said. *Don't name them.* Meg had a distinct feeling she was never ordering veal in a restaurant again. "Where's his mama?"

"He's his mama's first calf. She didn't appreciate the trouble he caused her and rejected him. One of the wranglers spotted the mama kicking at him when he tried to nurse."

"Oh, the poor thing."

The hurt in her heart for the little guy must have shown on her face. Adam pushed away from the wall and gave her a reassuring smile. "It happens sometimes. As of right now he's being bottle-fed."

The calf scrambled to his feet and crossed to where Adam had squatted on his haunches. The way the new calf nudged at Adam's fingers, she knew he was searching for food, and her heart twisted for the little orphan.

Spreading his fingers in front of the calf, Adam let him suck on a few. "He ate just a little bit ago so he doesn't actually need anything, but he's comforted by the sucking."

For Meg everything seemed so surreal. Just a few days ago she'd moved into a spacious Uptown Dallas condo and was counting the hours until she'd be sharing it with her new husband.

Her only complaint about her life in the big city was getting from point A to point B in the middle of Dallas's famed four-hour-long rush hour. Now she stood in a country barn where the word *traffic* had no meaning, never mind *rush hour*, along with a baby cow and a baby horse and a man who looked like he belonged in a western movie, wearing a white hat and saving the day.

But the one thing she found most surprising? Not working as a waitress, not living in a single room, not buying clothing from two sisters who apparently didn't have real names or not having a traditional Sunday family dinner in the middle of true God's country. *No.* For the better part of the last two days and most certainly from the second she'd walked in the Farraday front door—until this moment—she hadn't given Jonathan Cox more than a passing thought. As angry as she was at the asshole for what he'd done and for the mess he'd gotten her into, she hurt more for that poor little calf losing the love of his mama than she did for herself. How could she not feel anything?

Granted, she was still pissed off as all hell and maybe even a little scared. Okay, a lot scared. But she'd have thought she'd be at least a tiny bit sad, depressed, heartbroken. The only feeling that emerged when she thought of Jonathan was the urge to break his neck. What did that say about the supposed man of her dreams? And why was she even slightly concerned that, with all this hay, if she bumped against Adam again, the arcing electricity might set the place on fire?

• • •

"So what do you think?" Sean Farraday gazed out the backdoor window.

Brooks looked up from his cup of coffee. "About what?"

The Farraday family patriarch glanced over his shoulder at his son. "Surely you can't be that dense?"

"I beg your pardon?"

"The woman. Meg. And your brother."

Dark brows that mirrored his own rose high on Brooks's forehead. Often in large families every child was a little different, a unique combination of maternal and paternal genetics that produced tall, short, thin, heavy, dark-haired, blonde and other diverse appearances. Then you had families like Sean's. There was no mistaking a Farraday son. Or daughter.

"Meg seems nice enough, but I wouldn't use her name and Adam's in the same sentence."

"Don't know." Sean returned his gaze to the land outside. His boys were all getting older, and not a single one showed any sign of settling down. Not that his sons lived like hermits but Sean had yet to see any one woman remain in any of his sons' lives for more than a short while.

Since his wife had passed, working alongside his boys, watching them grow into strong and faithful men, had been the greatest joy of his life. He'd hate to think that any of them would miss out on what he and Helen had. The idea that even one of the boys might fail to find a mate and settle down was beginning to rattle him. Badly.

But, with this little redhead, Sean saw a fire in his eldest son's eyes when he looked at that young woman that Sean had yet to see in any of his sons, and it gave Sean a sliver of hope. It wasn't good for these strapping men to be alone. And this little gal was as Irish as they came. Sean suspected there was a temper to go with the hair. Like his Helen, fiery was good. In many ways. But, as much as he liked Meg, his gut said something was seriously off, and he hoped, whatever it was, it wouldn't mean trouble for any of his boys.

CHAPTER EIGHT

One hip on the corner of the old oak desk, D.J. faced Reed, the officer on duty. "Tell me-again exactly what happened. And don't leave out a single detail."

"A guy came in. Flashed a PI badge in my face and snapped the flap shut so fast, if I'd actually tried to read it, my nose would have wound up in his pocket."

"What exactly did he want?"

"He had a photo of the new waitress. Said she's wanted for questioning in an FBI investigation."

"Did he happen to say why he's looking for her?"

Reed shrugged. "Did a nice job of evading the question. But judging by the late-model Jaguar he drove up in, someone is willing to spend big bucks to find her."

When D.J. had run the plates on Meg yesterday for Adam, nothing had come up on her for any priors or outstanding warrants. If it's true she's part of some bigger investigation, that would take some deeper digging for him to uncover. "What did you tell him?"

"That he was welcome to leave a copy of the photo here along with his contact information. If she passed through these parts, we'd give him a call."

Interesting that, after only two days, just about everyone in town, including Reed, had developed a ring of protection around its newest resident. No one seeming to care who she was, where she came from or how long she'd be staying. "Did he leave his contact info?"

Reed handed D.J. an embossed business card. The officer was right about one thing: somebody didn't care what it cost to track down Meg O'Brien.

Address was out of San Antonio. Meg's car was registered in

Dallas. A background check on the PI firm was in order. It didn't take a genius to figure out something was out of kilter with this entire scenario. Meg seemed to be a nice girl. She really did. But that she had zero experience in the world of waitressing was obvious to any fool.

From the way she handled herself at the supper table, D.J. would bet the ranch that the woman would have had no problem sitting down to dine with the president of the United States. She'd probably have better manners than him to boot. Her back was rod straight. She never once leaned into her plate; her fork always came all the way to her mouth. The napkin had found its way onto her lap the moment she'd sat down, and, when she wasn't cutting her food, her other wrist remained at rest on her lap. Meg wasn't putting on airs or practicing sixth-grade cotillion lessons. This was habit. So that left the questions: who was she for real and why was someone looking for her?

• • •

The genuine wonder in Meg's eyes as they'd visited with the new colt and calf made Adam smile from the inside out. Every time he dealt with new life, that same sense of marvel overcame him. Nothing about the miracle of life was mundane or ordinary, and he'd really enjoyed seeing that reflected in Meg's every reaction. Walking back to the house, he had to shove his hands in his pockets to resist reaching over to hold her hand.

"I don't suppose"—Meg slowed her pace—"there's a library or Internet café in town?"

From the way one side of her face scrunched as she asked, he had the feeling she was already well aware of the answer to that one. "'Fraid not. There's a county library in Butler Springs."

Her brows pleated, and her lips slid tightly between her teeth.

"What are you needing?"

"I … haven't had a chance to … call home. I, … uh, lost my cell and was hoping to send an email until I can get a new phone."

"Abbie has Wi-Fi at the café. If you have existing service, I think the sisters sell phones."

Stopping short, Meg swirled in his direction, her arms spread wide, her palms face up. "Do they have real names?"

Adam swallowed a hard laugh, spewing air from the sides of his mouth like a blacksmith's bellow. "Aunt Eileen probably knows the answer. But, for as long as I can remember, they've owned that shop, and everyone has called them Sissy and Sister."

"Any other siblings?" Meg moved forward again.

"Nope. Just the two of them." Nearly at the back door, he pulled his phone from his pocket. "You're welcome to call home if you'd like."

Nibbling at one corner of her mouth, Meg stared at the phone so long and hard, he wondered what the hell was going on with her.

"Is there a problem?" he ventured, afraid to push too hard and fracture the easy rapport they'd shared in the barn.

"No. No. Thank you." Tentative fingers took the phone in hand.

He watched her punch *67 and then dial. So she didn't want her family, or whoever she was calling, to see his phone number. He would have to ask D.J. to dig a little further into Meg's life. It was one thing to not want to deal with the man she didn't marry. And there was nothing too terribly odd about needing some distance from said man—but avoiding family? He couldn't imagine not contacting his dad or brothers if he were in trouble.

Meg took a few steps to one side, off the path, holding the phone to one ear, her finger in the other. He was torn between affording her the privacy she clearly wanted and gleaning whatever information he could about this unique woman. Her shoulders hunched as though creating a protective wall, and he knew, whether she wanted to or not, she was now talking to someone back home.

• • •

"Mom, it's me. I've only got a minute. I want you to know all is well. I'm doing fine. Please don't look for me. Tell Dad not to send out the troops. I just need a little time. Love you." Meg hung up as fast as she could. Not that anyone was tracing calls, but she didn't really understand how this sort of thing worked, and she simply didn't want to be found. Not yet. Straightening her spine, she turned to face Adam again. The man was too damn handsome for his own good. Or for hers.

Hell, all three brothers were cast from the same mold. Dark wavy hair, dreamy eyes and strong square jaws, all packaged in six-foot-plus muscular frames. No weaklings among the Farradays. Even the dad—the only difference between Sean Farraday and his sons were the strands of gray peppered in his hair and the deep lines feathering out from the corners of his eyes. This was a man who had worked hard in the outdoors and had not been afraid to laugh at what life handed him.

But it was Adam's smile that sent butterflies fluttering in her stomach, had her palms going damp and the tingle of anticipation skittering up her spine. She needed to get a grip and focus on her situation. Sooner than later she would return to Dallas, and Adam Farraday would be nothing more than a memory. A very vivid memory. Stepping back onto the path, she extended her arm, holding the cell phone out to him.

"Did you get a hold of someone?" Adam slid the phone back into his pocket and pivoted around toward the house, waited for her to fall in step beside him.

"Voice mail." She knew perfectly well her mother was unlikely to answer a call if she didn't recognize the number. And an unidentified caller marked Private was immediately ignored.

"I left a message. I'll visit the sisters tomorrow after work. See about getting a new phone."

The two ladies seemed to have everything a town resident could want. If Adam was mistaken about the phones, she could try the hardware store. Assuming every cop show on TV didn't have it wrong, those prepaid disposable phones were impossible to trace. For now, she liked those odds.

"Hey, Dad." Adam followed Meg into the kitchen. "Where's Brooks?"

Before Sean Farraday could answer, Aunt Eileen came in from the hall, holding up a deck of cards. "It seems we've lost another player. The Chapman's youngest fell from a tree. They think his arm is broken. Brooks is on his way over."

"He's making a house call?" Good heavens, this place truly was a throwback in time.

"It's on his way to town," Adam's father explained. "If it's something Brooks can handle without an X-ray, then he'll save everyone a trip. Otherwise they'll go to the hospital in Butler Springs to get it X-rayed and set."

"That's pretty far for a broken arm."

"Someday he's going to have a setup like Adam here, everything the town needs under one roof. But right now we have more animals in these parts than people."

"Just how big is Tuckers Bluff?"

"We've got over five hundred families. Over three thousand people. And we have the school too."

"*The* school?"

Eileen lifted her chin with pride. "Tucker Independent School District. Serves grades kindergarten through twelve for Tuckers Bluff and two smaller nearby communities."

Adam leaned into her and whispered, "One building."

"I heard that. The new high school will be ready next fall." Eileen speared her nephew with a sideways glance, then turned to Meg. "Are you up for a little card game and some pie?"

"Oh, I don't know." Meg could feel the calories making themselves at home on her hips as she eyed the homemade dessert. "I have to be up awfully early for my shift tomorrow."

"Made them myself this afternoon," Eileen enticed.

"Eileen's blueberry pies take the blue ribbon at the fair every year. Best this side of the Mississippi." The way Sean Farraday beamed, anyone would think he'd baked the pies himself.

"Maybe one slice and a quick game," Meg agreed, "until Brooks comes back."

"Oh, he's not coming back." Eileen set a deck of cards on the table beside the pie. "Adam here'll drive you home." Grabbing a knife from a nearby drawer, Aunt Eileen grinned up at her nephew. "You don't mind, do you? Since you're both going in the same direction."

Adam's shoulders stiffened, and the easy smile of earlier shifted into something more formal, plastic. "No, ma'am. Don't mind at all."

So why did Meg get the distinct impression that Adam Farraday would rather have played with a scorpion than ride thirty minutes into town—again—with her?

CHAPTER NINE

"Your aunt should play Vegas." Meg clipped her seat belt into place. "Did she lose a single round?"

"Not likely. The only card player better than her is my dad, and it's been years since I've seen him take more than a token pot."

"It was like she knew what cards we had."

"She probably did. Aunt Eileen and the Tuckers Bluff Ladies' Afternoon Social Club have had a Saturday morning card game at the café for as long as I can remember."

"I saw them yesterday." Meg frowned. "But a few of those ladies didn't seem that old."

"Nope. The group shifts from time to time. Sally May Henderson and Dorothy Wilson are founding members. Those two and my aunt Eileen would have to be on death's doorstep to miss a game. Nora Brown is the youngest official member. She doesn't miss a Saturday game."

"How many women are in the club?"

"Hard to say. Folks come and go. The last ten years the county has been growing rather than shrinking. Though the club's purpose seems to have shifted to focus more on the social part. The ladies were more active when I was a kid as most of the moms stayed at home. In those days they had all sorts of community-based activities. Anything from fund-raising for what's now the local school to a quilting bee. Whenever someone had a new baby, they got a handmade quilt." Adam remembered how excited his mother had been when the club had worked on Grace's quilt. After six boys his mother had been over the moon to have a little girl. Even after all these years, his heart constricted at the many things his mom never got to see.

"You okay?" Meg twisted in her seat.

"What?"

"You grew quiet. Serious."

"Sorry."

Loosening her seat belt, she twisted fully, leaning back against the door and smiled. "Penny for your thoughts?"

Adam stared ahead at the gray pavement. Normally he would have diverted the conversation away from himself and his family, but instead he found himself wanting to share. "My sister, Grace's, quilt was the last one the social club did as a group. My mom developed an infection. It went septic. She died ten days after Grace's birth."

"Now I'm sorry. How old were you?"

"Twelve."

Lips pressed tightly together, Meg didn't say a word at first. "Is that why your aunt Eileen lives at the ranch?"

Adam nodded. "She's Mom's sister. Arrived the week before Grace was born and has been here for us every day since."

"I know we only spent one afternoon together, but I like your aunt. Now I think I like her even more."

"Can't imagine what our lives would have been like if she hadn't been here. Grace would probably have grown up to be a wrangler if it were left up to the Farraday men."

"Well, if you think about it, with a law degree, she'll just be doing a different sort of wrangling."

From deep in his belly, a laugh erupted. Meg had said just the right thing to snap him out of the melancholy moment. "I have to admit, I'm looking forward to the first lawyer who tangles with my sister. She may be the runt of the family, but she's a fireball."

"It must be the Irish." Meg eyes sparked with a kindred understanding.

"With that red hair, you would know. Tell me about your parents. Are they both Irish?"

Meg shook her head. "Only my father. I get the red hair and fiery temper from him."

"So you do have a temper?"

A rosy flush filled her cheeks. "If you push me too far."

He resisted the urge to shift in his seat to make a little more room in his jeans and instead wondered what it might be like to push Meg O'Brien's buttons.

• • •

Though it wasn't much past sunset when they pulled up to the café, all the lights were off, and the restaurant was clearly closed.

"Sundays are Abbie's only day off," Adam explained.

"But she opened this morning."

Adam nodded and pulling into a space by the back door, shifted the truck into Park. "Some folks come in and eat after church. Not a big crowd. A few folks will come early for breakfast and then head out to church. But, by midafternoon, the place is empty, and Abbie goes home."

"One afternoon doesn't seem like enough rest for anyone."

"A lot of folks around here would agree with you. She works seven days a week from opening to close and has ever since she bought the place a few years back."

"She probably doesn't take vacations either, does she?" Creaky wheels were turning in the back of Meg's mind. Everyone needed downtime.

"Can't say that she has." Adam slid out of the driver's seat and circled around to Meg's side before she could climb out. "Here, let me give you a hand."

Much the same words had been spoken when she'd crawled out of the massive vehicle in her wedding gown, but that short time ago she'd still been spitting mad at Jonathan Cox and had barely noticed the strong hands gripping her waist, lifting her slowly to solid ground. "Thank you."

"You settled in okay? Need anything?"

Lifting the bag of leftovers Aunt Eileen had insisted she bring home, Meg shook her head, chuckling. "I think your aunt forgot I live over a restaurant. I've got enough food here to last me till the next millennium."

Adam's lips curved into that lazy smile that made her stomach do somersaults. "She does like to feed people. But I meant upstairs." He pointed to the cafe's second floor. "I know it's used more for storage than anything else. You comfortable enough?"

"More than enough." The place didn't compare to the beautiful condo she'd left behind. It had taken her months to pick out just the right pieces for each room. In the end she had an eclectic blend of traditional and modern. The perfect combination for a young couple living in the heart of the city. And yet, after only a couple of days of simple country living, surrounded by cows and horses, and handsome men in jeans and Stetsons, the sleek uptown locale seemed to be rapidly losing its appeal.

And now, reflecting on the condo, she realized she had one more thing to uncover—whose name and money had been used to purchase the contemporary uptown loft. Every time she thought of what Jonathan had done, and what it might mean for her and her family, her jaw clenched tight enough to crack a molar.

"You okay?" Adam leaned forward, feet slightly spread, right hand midway between them. He looked poised to spring into emergency action if she were to start foaming at the mouth or burst a blood vessel.

Both equally possible if she continued to focus on her asshole ex-fiancé. "Sorry. Just thinking about taking out the trash."

"I see." Adam stepped back. "Be sure to let me know if you need any help with heavy lifting."

An image of Adam holding appearance-conscious Jonathan Cox high overhead like a set of competition barbells popped into Meg's mind as clear as the man standing in front of her, looking more confused with her every thought. She held back a grin. "I certainly will. Promise."

Apparently satisfied, Adam nodded. "I'll walk you up. It's still kind of early, but I bet you're about ready to hit the sack ..." The man's big blue eyes rounded like a pair of decorative

Halloween eyeballs. "I mean—"

Meg held up her hand. This time she let her smile show. "I know what you meant. And walking me all the way up stairs isn't necessary."

"Tell that to my father and Aunt Eileen." Completely ignoring her protest, he dropped his hand along the small of her back and ushered her forward.

Through her layers of clothing, she could feel the warm press of his hand. She had to force herself to push ahead and not lean back into his strength. Suddenly standing on her own two feet felt like more work than she was up to. But leaning on Adam Farraday was totally out of the question. No matter how many sparks and tingles made themselves at home whenever he was near. She wasn't trusting another man with anything again. Ever.

At the top of the stairs she used the key Abbie had given her to unlock the door. "Thank you for the ride."

"My pleasure." He showed no sign of moving. For a split second she wondered if he was waiting for an invitation inside. Though the way he tipped his head back slightly, she realized he was merely waiting for her to go inside and close the door.

Country manners. She could certainly grow accustomed to this. Smiling at him, she eased the door to a closed position, not really wanting to place the hard wooden barrier between them. The second the latch sounded, she scrambled through the obstacle course of boxes and scattered furniture to perch near the front window, waiting for the engine of the huge pickup to roar to life and the headlights to cut through the dark night. Her gaze remained on the white truck as it pulled away from the café, did an about-face, and, leaving the lot, cut across the narrow road and pulled into his own drive. Telling herself that her making sure he got home safely was no different than him safely seeing her home, she kept her gaze trained on the clinic. And this year summer in Texas would be cool and breezy. Right.

• • •

Dead tired and yet wide awake, Adam dragged his butt up the stairs of his clinic to his private quarters. The ride home had been pleasant and much more lighthearted than he'd expected. At first Meg seemed tense, nervous, almost scared. He'd made it a point to stay away from the burning questions: where was she from, why had she appeared in the middle of the night like a statuesque angel and why was she settling into small-town life instead of hurrying home to the big city? By the time they'd reached town, she'd been smiling and chatting with him as though they'd been neighbors all their lives.

Somehow along the way they'd shared favorite colors: Meg's was blue. Favorite foods? Meg was a sucker for anything pumpkin flavored. Especially if it had something to do with vanilla ice cream. But he hadn't learned anything more revealing about this woman who appeared in his world out of nowhere. No hint as to the reasons for the wedding dress or why she'd been driving on an out-of-the-way road in the middle of nowhere. Spending this little bit of time alone had done nothing to squash his doubts that she was hiding from someone or something. Every passing minute alone with this striking redhead had only left him incredibly more curious.

CHAPTER TEN

Monday afternoon Meg had bought a disposable prepaid cell phone and then stayed up way too late last night surfing the Net on it. Tracking down each of her and Jonathan's joint accounts had proven more challenging than she'd expected. Most of the passwords had been changed, and the ones that hadn't been had painted a miserable portrait of her financial situation.

She didn't understand why all but one of her accounts had been siphoned by her ex. Even though it was her money, since childhood the account had been in her and her father's name. More than likely that was the only thing that had saved it from Jonathan's greedy hands. But that still left her wondering, if Jonathan had used her credit cards for his various extravagances, what the hell had he done with all the rest of her savings? She'd longed, more than once, for a real keyboard, a full-size screen and a printer.

Unscrambling her finances was only part of her predicament. She needed to keep tabs on what was happening back home. Hopefully Google Alerts would help her determine when it would be safe to return. Since she'd yet to figure out any way to access her only viable bank account without tipping off her family as to her whereabouts, she'd have to rely on her waitress wages to take care of the astronomical mechanic's bill staring her down.

● ● ●

Eileen Callahan glided through the door of the café, waving. "Don't you look pretty as a picture."

"Thank you. In for a late breakfast?"

"Oh, no. It's Tuesday."

Meg nodded. If yesterday was Monday, then today was indeed Tuesday.

"The rest of the girls should be here any minute. I'll have a cup of coffee and a piece of Frank's apple pie while I'm waiting." Eileen shook out of her jacket and sauntered to the same table she's been at when Meg had arrived in town last week.

From behind the counter Abbie waved at the Farraday matriarch. "You going to have some of Frank's pie today?"

"Already ordered it from Meg." Eileen pointed at Meg with her thumb. "Good little waitress you got here, Abbie. Hope you know it."

Abbie laughed at the older woman. "If I don't, I'm dumber than donkey dung."

The two women laughed some more, and, despite the unpleasant analogy, Meg smiled too. In a balancing act Meg carried the pie plate and coffee cup for Eileen with one arm and the carafe to refill other customers' morning brew with her other hand. A disproportionate sense of accomplishment had her grinning broadly that she'd made it all the way to Eileen's table without sending the dishes crashing to the floor.

"Sorry I'm late." A petite older woman with curly brown hair and a bounce in her step sidled in beside Eileen. "Stopped at the clinic. One of these days Becky will learn to hem her own pants."

"At least you have a granddaughter who needs you." Eileen dug into the freshly baked pie.

"Yeah, well, I suppose," the other woman agreed reluctantly.

Meg had been running a little crazy when the ladies had played cards on Saturday. There was no way she would remember this woman's name. "What will you have this morning?"

"I'd love a piece of that pie. Apple is Frank's best."

"Another apple pie coming up." Meg slid the pad into her apron and spun on her heel. By the time she'd served up another slice, the back table was buzzing with chatter and activity. And cards. Apparently the regular Saturday morning poker game also consisted of the occasional weekday morning game. Though Meg suspected having a new waitress in town might have been a contributing factor to this particular Tuesday morning's game.

A couple of hours later when Adam came through the café door, Meg was running at full speed, trying to keep up with the customers. He looked around at the crowded tables, and it warmed Meg's heart to see his smile spread when he spotted his aunt. From the pile of poker chips in front of Eileen Callahan, the woman was on a winning streak. Yet her maternal instincts must have kicked in because, just as Adam's gaze landed on her, Eileen glanced up to return the smile.

Adam's attention shifted from his aunt to the counter Meg was wiping down and flashed that winning smile at her. She almost lost her breath. Surely that smile was registered somewhere as a lethal weapon. He probably had a trail of broken hearts strewed across town. She could feel the instant heat rushing in her veins.

Swinging one leg across to straddle the stool in front of her, Adam reached for a nearby menu. Meg wasn't sure why. Everyone who came in seemed to have every item memorized.

"Lunching by yourself today?" Now why did she ask that? Who he had lunch with was none of her business.

"Only have time to pick up takeout for the office."

"Oh, I'll check if it's ready." She shifted about to hit the kitchen when his hand shot up to stop her.

"No need. I didn't phone in the order."

"Oh." She bobbed her head. "Well, tell me what can I get you, and I'll have Frank put a rush on it."

He flashed that power-watt grin again, and she had to bite her cheek to stop herself from beaming back at him. She scribbled down his order and served him an iced tea while he waited for the food. Meg did her best to go about her work as if he weren't there, but how does anyone ignore a man like Adam Farraday and the things that smile did to her?

"How are you holding up?" he asked when she came behind

the counter to make a fresh pot of coffee.

"Not bad."

"You seem to be getting the hang of it."

She dropped the prepackaged grounds into the machine and turned to fully face him. "The hardest part is learning everyone's names. There isn't a person in here who Abbie doesn't know."

"She's lived in Tuckers Bluff a lot longer than you have." Adam shrugged.

"I know but still …"

"Maybe I can help." He set aside his drink and curled his finger for Meg to lean in closer. "Whose name don't you know?"

"Well …" She bit her lip and looked around. The tables were thinning out, and she'd caught quite a few names. "The women playing cards with your aunt. The one with curly brown hair?"

"Dorothy Wilson. Her granddaughter Becky works for me."

Meg nodded her head. "And the woman next to her is Nora, right?"

Smiling again, Adam nodded. "That's right."

"She likes unsweetened tea with Splenda."

"See? You're doing great. Even if I haven't a clue what she likes to drink."

This time she did return the grin. One of the things that had always made her stand out at any hotel she'd ever worked at was her ability to remember names. Both her employees' and the clientele's. Just normally not all at once. "Thanks. I'm sure trying."

The bell dinged in the kitchen, and Meg knew that had to be Adam's order. As much as she would have liked to visit a little longer, she pushed away from the counter and scurried back to pick up the full brown paper bag.

"You got that, honey?" Abbie looked up from taking an order at a tableful of teenage girls.

"No problem." Meg had worked the register a few times this morning, and it was pretty straightforward.

Adam followed her to the end of the counter. It only took her a few seconds to ring up the meals while he fished his wallet from his back pocket. She tried not to stare, but it was pretty hard not to notice the fit of his jeans. In Dallas she'd have guessed that was the body of a man who worked out at the gym. And often. But here, she had the feeling those toned muscles came from sheer hard work.

"Here you go." Holding a few bills, his hand stretched forward. The barest of touches as she retrieved the money from his palm was all it took for the same sparks that had skittered up her back at dinner the other night to make another appearance. The way his eyes briefly widened and his nostrils flared, it was a safe guess that he'd felt the same shock.

A flush of heat rose to her cheeks, and she almost pressed her hands to her face in a futile effort to cool down. Placing the money in the drawer, she slid the bag in front of Adam. "I hope everyone enjoys it."

"We will." He set his hat on his head and, touching the brim with one hand, gave a quick dip of his chin. "Thank you again."

She kept her eyes on him as he walked out the door. As he made his way across the street, she realized she was staring. Sucking in a deep breath, she turned her attention back to the coffeepot. There were other things for her to do than daydream over a good-looking cowboy, like check in on that group of teens. Fresh coffee ready to go, she grabbed the carafe and, doing her best to clear her mind of Adam Farraday, made the rounds, starting with the poker-playing table.

Cards in hand, the ladies at the table grew surprisingly quiet as Meg approached. "Anyone like some more coffee? Nora, more tea?"

Several heads bobbed. Eileen was the first to speak. "I see Adam came in to get lunch for the clinic."

That seemed pretty obvious. Meg nodded.

"Pretty unusual." Dorothy lifted a handful of poker chips. "I'll see you and raise you five."

"I'm out." Nora dropped her cards on the table. "I always

thought something would come of him and Becky. You know, the way they always seem to be teasing each other. Pretty friendly for a boss and his employee."

Tempted to look out the window again and wondering how much truth there was to Nora's observations, Meg filled Nora's glass next.

"Don't be silly," Eileen added, tossing a few chips into the pot. "Whole town knows Becky's been in love with my Ethan since she was two feet tall."

"And your Ethan has yet to smarten up and know what a good catch my girl is." Dorothy laid down her cards and grinned. "Houseful of ladies."

Everyone at the table groaned as Meg filled the last cup and moved on to another table. This time she did let her gaze drift over to the large plate-glass windows and settle on the veterinary clinic across the street. With all she had to deal with, she didn't need to add one handsome-as-sin cowboy to the mix. Hadn't she already learned her lesson? The last thing she needed was a man. Especially one who made her senses reel and her breath hitch. No, Adam Farraday was a really bad idea.

CHAPTER ELEVEN

"How's she working out?" Perched on a counter stool, Becky pointed her chin at Meg.

Abbie refilled her nearly empty glass of sweet tea. "Catching on. She's a fast learner."

"She does seem to fit in." All this week and last, since watching Meg scurry about on her first day, Becky had meant to come by and properly introduce herself to the new waitress, but one day had rolled into the next and so on down the line until now. Since the waitress herself had proven to be excellent at avoiding personal questions and still staying friendly, gossip around town was flying with all sorts of speculation. According to Ned she'd arrived at his shop almost two weeks ago at the crack of dawn wearing a wedding dress and left it stuffed in the trash can. From there things got a bit sketchy.

One faction insisted she'd been left at the altar by her high school sweetheart. Another group seemed to think she'd run off on a billionaire fiancé old enough to be her grandfather. And yet a few more seemed to think she'd made it through the ceremony and gotten cold feet on her wedding night and that her new husband was scouring every big city in the state looking for her. Becky had to laugh at that last one. Like there was such a thing as a virginal bride on her wedding night.

"Hash smothered and covered and pull the pork." Behind the counter, Meg smiled at Frank, the cook, and slapped the order onto the stick. With the ease of someone who had worked a country café for years, she grabbed the coffeepot and made the rounds, filling cups and making chitchat with the regulars.

"Certainly seems more certain of herself than she was last week," Becky agreed.

"And the place has never been busier. I've even got curious folks from neighboring towns coming in for lunch. Don't know how long she's staying, but I'm not complaining." A couple of guys Becky didn't recognize flagged Abbie down. "Gotta go. Like I said, business is great."

"There you are." Kelly, the clinic receptionist, stood beside Becky, glancing around for an empty booth or table.

Things were always pretty slow at the vet clinic on the days Adam made his ranch calls, so today she and Kelly decided to do a little honest-to-goodness fact-finding.

"Sorry it took me so long. I swear Ms. Peabody needs to find a man. Maybe if she had something else to keep her busy, she wouldn't be such a hypochondriac with her pets."

"Never happen." Becky grabbed her tea and followed Kelly to a nearby table. "Even when Mr. Peabody was alive, whatever ailed Nadine seemed to afflict one of her animals. Dealing with her on an almost daily basis is as much a fact of life as death and taxes."

"Still—"

"Afternoon, ladies." Meg appeared tableside with menus tucked under her arm. Waiting a moment for the two to settle in, she set a glass of water in front of each of them along with the menus. "Today's special is pot roast with carrots and skinny potatoes—"

"Skinny?" Kelly asked. "That's new."

Meg laughed. "Instead of cut in chunks, Frank sliced them like steak fries and is calling them skinny potatoes. My guess is he's hoping the power of suggestion will counteract the calories."

The two coworkers both laughed, but Kelly was the one to say, "If only."

Pad and pen in hand, Meg looked to Kelly first. "Would you like something else to drink?"

"No." She sighed. "Until I lose my birthday pounds, it will be water for me."

"Birthday pounds?" Meg frowned, and Becky rolled her eyes.

"Yeah." Kelly blew out another heavy sigh. "I sort of ate

almost the whole cake all by myself. And the cupcakes Abbie made too."

Shaking her head, Becky reached for the menu. "I'd kill for a few of those curves you're complaining about."

Casually Meg eyed Becky, then shifted her scrutiny to Kelly. The clinic receptionist had porcelain skin, a smile worthy of toothpaste commercials, big brown eyes with long thick lashes and a full guitarlike figure that should make real men drool.

Sticking the pen behind her ear, Meg hefted a lazy shrug. "No one asked me, but I think you're both nuts. Be right back."

"See?" Becky leaned forward, clearly enunciating the single syllable word. "You are not fat."

"We're not here to discuss me." Kelly pushed aside the menu. "We're supposed to find out about *her*."

"Agreed."

Two minutes later Meg reappeared, ready to take their orders.

"So," Kelly started, "how are you liking it here, Meg?"

"Fine, thank you. Abbie's a great boss." Pen in hand, she smiled. "You ladies ready to order?"

"Cobb salad please." Kelly proceeded with her questions before Meg could finish writing. "Have you always been a waitress?"

Meg offered a noncommittal grunt before lifting her gaze from the pad to Kelly. "Would you like some grilled chicken with that? A little extra protein keeps me from feeling hungry in the middle of the afternoon."

"Great idea. Thanks." Kelly shot Becky a frustrated glance.

"What about you?" Meg turned to Becky.

"I'd like the bacon cheddar cheeseburger with a side of slaw and fried onion rings."

Meg chuckled. "Gotta love a girl with a healthy appetite."

"I certainly have that. And, by the way, my name is Becky. This is Kelly."

"Nice to meet you both."

Meg's grin grew a little wider, her stance a little more

relaxed, and Becky suddenly felt a spike of guilt for prying.

Meg slid the pad into her pocket. "I'll have those orders right out."

Waiting a few seconds for Meg to reach the kitchen, Becky blew out a soft sigh. "I don't think we'll have any better luck getting answers than the rest of the town has."

Kelly's gaze settled on Meg across the cafe. "Looks that way."

By the time Kelly had finished her salad and Becky had shoveled down her burger, most of the lunch crowd had cleared out.

"I just want to mention for the record, one more time"—Kelly tossed her napkin on the table—"I think it is horribly unfair that you can eat like a starving teenage boy and still look like a twig."

"And there's the problem. The grass is always greener on the other side. While you long to see Olive Oyl in the mirror, I'd prefer not to be associated with anything that reminds a man of a teenage boy."

"A man? Or Ethan Farraday?"

Becky hated that just about everyone in the town, except for maybe the new waitress, knew that in the first grade she'd fallen head over light-up sneakers in love with Ethan Farraday. "Ethan is on the other side of the world. He's probably got a woman in every port."

"That's the navy. He's a marine."

Becky rolled her eyes. "That's not the point. I'm not in elementary school anymore."

"Right."

Once again Meg appeared, pad and pen in hand. "Is anyone up for some desert?"

"No, thanks. Nothing more for me." Kelly patted her tummy as though she'd eaten more than a salad for lunch.

"Actually"—Becky turned to Meg—"a few of us go out once a month or so on Friday nights. Nothing special. Just us girls, maybe a movie or dinner. We'd love for you to join us."

"Sometimes we'll go over to the Boot 'N' Scoots in Butler Springs."

"Boots 'N' Scoots?" Meg asked.

"Country bar. Good place for a little two-stepping," Becky explained. "Tonight we're just going to hang out at Donna's, keep her company while she's on bed rest. Play a little cards maybe or watch a good chick flick."

"Oh." Meg's eyes darted between the two of them. "I, uh …" Her gaze shifted out the window, across the way to the clinic, then back again. "You work across the street, don't you?"

"Yeah, I do. You don't have anything against animals, do you?" Becky asked, her tone teasing.

"Oh, no. No. Not at all. I think that would be nice. Thank you."

"Great." Kelly slapped her hands together. "Here's Donna's address. It's not far. You can walk—"

"Or I can give you a ride if you like," Becky offered. "But I'm going over early to help get the place ready."

Meg accepted the small piece of paper Kelly handed her, read it over, then folded and slid it into her pocket. "I'm sure I can find my way."

"Good," Becky said. "Consider this your official welcome to Tuckers Bluff."

Meg smiled, but Becky saw way too much apprehension in the woman's eyes. Maybe the faction who believed Meg had a ticked-off husband scouring Texas for his runaway bride weren't that far off the mark after all.

● ● ●

Wow. A night out with the girls. Another surprise about small-town living. Meg had expected to be ignored or to be on the receiving end of a had-to-have-been-born-here-to-be-accepted sort of attitude from the locals. Instead everyone seemed to go out of their way to make her feel at home. Welcome. Standing by the empty table, a dish in each hand, she watched the laughing coworkers cut across the parking lot.

She'd learned a little about the girls from the conversations over poker games at the Silver Spurs. Becky Wilson had worked at the veterinary clinic since high school and had been crushing on Ethan Farraday since grade school. According to her grandmother, Ethan was a blind fool for never noticing his baby sister's best friend was the catch of a lifetime.

Kelly, friends with Grace Farraday and Becky since childhood, had left town to attend the University of Texas with no plans of returning to small-town life. In her sophomore year her dad had had a stroke, and she'd hurried home to help care for him and had been here ever since. From what Meg gathered, the veterinary clinic hadn't needed a receptionist, but Adam had created the job especially for Kelly.

Apparently there was some truth to the myth that small towns took care of their own. In Meg's case they seemed to be taking care of strangers too.

"Shannon's youngest has come down with a fever." Abbie took the dishes from Meg's hands. "She's got to pick him up at school and drop him off at her mother's. Do you mind staying a little longer until she comes in?"

"No. Not at all." Meg liked having something to do besides scour the Internet for updates on Jonathan and her father. A little more work at the café, followed by a night with the girls—away from the Internet—was a good thing.

"Thanks." Abbie smiled. "I could handle it alone, but I guarantee you, the minute the fates learn I'm in here by myself, a bus of tourists on their way to Carlsbad will break down on our doorstep, and the blue-haired ladies will all realize they're suddenly famished."

Meg couldn't help but laugh at the thought of Abbie overrun by a busload of women, like those who starred in *The Golden Girls*, on a group tour to New Mexico. "Glad I could help."

Almost an hour later, the ketchup and mustard, along with the sugar dispensers, had all been refilled in anticipation of the dinner crowd. Abbie had just put on a fresh pot of coffee. "I'm taking a few minutes to go over tomorrow's menu with Frank. Can you keep an eye on the back table for me?"

"No problem." Meg put the last of the sugar dispensers in place when the overhead bell dinged, announcing another patron. It was hard not to recognize a Farraday. Especially Adam. The three brothers she'd met so far took command of a room the moment they crossed the threshold.

Cell phone in hand, Adam Farraday smiled at the screen. When he finally looked up, he caught Meg watching him. "Abbie has you working the dinner shift tonight?"

"No. Shannon's running a little late." Meg followed him to the booth past the cash register. "Can I start you off with something to drink?"

In a casual move that she'd seen every man do when coming into the café, Adam removed his hat and hung it on the pseudo rack rising between the booths. Well-worn jeans, broken-in boots and the requisite cowboy hat were standard attire in this part of the state.

"Coffee would be great. Black."

"Coming right up." Meg had to take a deep breath not to rush for the coffee or trip over her own feet along the way. It wasn't normal for the air in her lungs to seize at the sight of a man. No matter how handsome the Farradays were, Adam was just a nice guy. And she'd sworn off men. For good.

"Hey." Shannon scurried in the front door, rushing to the back room. "So sorry I'm late. Where's Abbie?"

"Kitchen with Frank."

"Give me five to freshen up and I'll take over."

Meg smiled, nodded and carried a cup of black coffee to booth number two.

The cup clanked against the table, and, still smiling, Adam lifted his gaze to Meg. "Thanks."

She'd seen him smile more than once at dinner on Sunday,

but this lighter grin seemed brighter somehow. "Got your girl on the phone?" Oh, Lord. Meg couldn't believe she'd just said that. How to sound like a jealous teen.

"No." Adam chuckled. "My brother Ethan is posting pictures on Instagram of him and his buddies. It's hard knowing he's overseas and so close to danger, but, when these ridiculous pictures show up on my newsfeed ..." Adam lifted his phone for her to see a near mirror image of the three Farraday siblings she'd already met, only this one had sandy-blond hair, taking a selfie with two other guys, all of their faces contorted from laughter.

"Does a heart good." She didn't even know Ethan Farraday, and yet she felt lighter seeing the three servicemen joking around and having fun.

"Okay." Shannon shot out from the back hall. "I'm on. Thanks again."

Across the café, Shannon made the rounds, checking on the patrons, filling drinks and orders as needed.

"Care to join me for a cup?" Adam glanced up at her, his eyes still dancing with laughter.

At the same moment her mind screamed, "Danger, Will Robinson!" her head bobbed, and her mouth mumbled, "Thank you."

"Here's another." Adam continued to grin and held the phone out to her. She had to admit, Ethan looked like a college kid having a blast at a frat party. But she suspected a big part of the reason for the close-up selfies with no room for any backdrop was to avoid showing friends and family, or even enemies, where the soldiers were. For a few minutes at a time, it was easy for loved ones to forget their sons, or daughters, were in the line of fire in the most unstable corners of the world.

● ● ●

Adam did his best to mask the frantic beat of his heart with a huge smile and the sea of photos coming his way from Ethan. He hadn't meant to invite Meg to sit with him; the words had simply tumbled from his lips. No warning. No forethought. The only thing more surprising than his invitation was her easy acceptance. Not that he ever had trouble getting a girl, but he'd expected this one to be a bit more skittish under the circumstances. Maybe he'd been giving her too wide a berth. Maybe he didn't have to treat her with kid gloves. Except now that he had her across from him, he didn't have a clue where to start. "How are you liking the job?"

"More than I thought I would. Took a few days for my feet to finally stop complaining."

"Were you able to get a phone?"

Meg nodded. "Yeah. I got the last one. I understand cell phones tend to get broken a lot when you work an oil rig. Apparently we're closer to some of the oil rig camps than Butler Springs. Sister says they sell out fast."

"True, though I don't know how much longer the sales booms from the camps will last."

"What do you mean?"

"What goes up, must come down. Slumps come and go. And some people think we have a doozy of an oil slump hammering down. Lots of those camps have already closed up shop. Roustabout companies are closing. Wives who used to stay home are looking for outside work. The sisters have been around a long time. They know how to weather slow times but not so with everyone."

"You're thinking of your brother? The one who works in oil?"

Adam shrugged. "Connor knows the score. He's been squirreling away his money while he can. His heart's in horses."

"You mentioned he wanted the neighbor's land."

"Sometimes he'd talk of eastern horse country. Virginia, Kentucky. Where grass is plentiful and breeders have a name. But the last few years it's become clear to us that Mr. Brennan's kin aren't interested in having anything to do with west Texas. That's when the idea of side-by-side ranches took root in Connor's mind."

Growing up Connor was always about the horses. When their

dad and the others rode fences or moved the herd, Connor stalked the wild mustangs. For a while, the family had thought they might have two veterinarians in the family, but, by Connor's first year in high school, it was clear that he was all about the breeding and training of the four-legged beauties.

But the type of operation Connor dreamed of required more capital than the Farraday ranch could provide. It was no surprise to the family that the fearless kid fascinated by the powerful and dangerous mustangs would turn to a dangerous job, like working an oil rig, to save money.

"He's socking away the cash, and hopefully he'll have enough saved by the time Brennan is ready to sell. But enough about my brother. What about you? Do you have any siblings?"

Meg shook her head. "Only child."

Somehow that didn't surprise him. "I can't imagine growing up in a house without at least one brother to drive you crazy."

"I don't know. You all look pretty sane to me."

"Maybe *now*." He laughed. "But, on more than one occasion when we were kids, any of my brothers were lucky to reach their next birthday."

"I think I would have liked to have had at least one brother."

"You can have one of mine."

Megan laughed until she coughed. "Sorry, but that wasn't what I had in mind."

"Hey, I've got them broken in. You get the easy part now."

The sound of Meg's laughter worked him like a soothing balm after a long work day. One he could easily get used to—if she were going to stay.

CHAPTER TWELVE

"What can I get you two?" Shannon angled her body closer to Adam and gave Meg a big old wink.

"Oh, I'm not staying." As if Meg weren't already the talk of the town, she didn't need to start people gossiping about her and Adam too. "I'm going to Donna's tonight."

"With the girls?" Shannon let her pad droop and pointed at Meg with her pen. "You let her know we miss her around here."

"I will." Placing one hand on the table for leverage as she slid out of the booth, Meg was startled to feel Adam's strong fingers curl around her wrist.

"You said you'd join me for a cup of coffee. All I've done is eat up your time, showing off my kid brother. Please stay a minute and take a break. You've got to be exhausted."

"I really should—"

Shannon winked again and cut her off. "I'll be right back with more coffee."

"Thanks, Shannon." Adam still had his fingers around Meg's wrist. "How are you getting to Donna's?"

"I thought I'd walk."

"After working all day on your feet? Why don't you let me give you a lift?"

Working every day this week, her endurance seemed to be building, but the idea of riding to Donna's instead of walking did hold a certain appeal.

"I promise I won't bite," he added.

"It's not that. I don't want to impose."

"Consider yourself not imposing. Besides, I promised Dad that I'd go over to the ranch tonight. Donna's house is on my way."

"If you're sure?"

"I'm sure. Now will you stay for that coffee?"

"I'll get it." Meg slid the rest of the way out of the booth and scooted across the café to the other side of the counter, where Shannon waited for a fresh pot to finish brewing.

"Honey," Shannon almost whispered, "if you lasso yourself a Farraday, you're going to have to give lessons. Half the grown women in town, single or married, would love to rope in one of those brothers."

"I'm not—"

Shaking her head, Shannon raised her hand, palm out. "I'm just saying, that's the most interest I've seen from a Farraday man in a female living anywhere near this town since high school. I don't know your story, but a girl could do a lot worse than Adam Farraday."

The urge to argue tickled the back of her throat, but Meg knew there was no point. "Thanks. I'll take the coffee."

Shannon spun on her heel, and Meg sucked in a long calming breath. She'd already done worse, but she wasn't looking for better; this was only a cup of coffee. And just to be sure she didn't forget, she repeated her *this is just a cup of coffee* mantra in her mind all the way back to the table. "Here you go."

"Thanks. I've probably already had a gallon of this stuff, but every cup still hits the spot."

"Rough day?"

"Not really. Pretty routine but I've been on the road since six this morning. There's a lot of miles to cover from ranch to ranch, and it's just not always practical to haul large animals into town for a shot or a foot infection as though they were a cat or dog."

"No. I imagine not." Meg took a long sip of the warm brew. She'd not eaten anything since breakfast, and her stomach protested. Loudly.

Adam frowned. "When was the last time you ate?"

"I grabbed a muffin this morning."

"I'm not one to give unwanted advice, but I have it on excellent authority that a muffin does not qualify for a meal substitute."

"I'll eat something when I go home." *Home*. The word surprised her. Not her room. Not the apartment. Home. Had she actually come to think of the maze upstairs as home?

"You promise?"

"Promise."

Adam took his time. He seemed to be rolling his next words around like a swill of coffee. "Want to tell me how you wound up outside Tuckers Bluff at the crack of dawn?"

She knew she had to stop avoiding this question sooner or later. "My wedding was ... canceled."

"Canceled?"

"Let's just say I found out what a conniving asshat my fiancé was before it was too late."

Adam didn't respond. Not a word, not a nod, not even a blink.

"I needed to clear my head, so I just got in the car and started driving. Hopped on the tollway, caught I-30 until it became I-20, and, the next thing I knew, I was halfway across Texas in the middle of the night. Took an exit, hoping to find a place to stay. Apparently roads with numbers out here aren't necessarily major thoroughfares."

This time Adam smiled and shook his head.

"So I kept going, thinking eventually the road would lead somewhere. But the tire had a different plan." Raising the cup to her lips, she breathed in the familiar aroma. "Did you ever find the dog?"

"Nope. I've been out there twice. Once in broad daylight and again after dark. No signs of an injured animal."

It made no sense that, in the middle of nowhere, a dog could simply appear and disappear. "I don't understand. I know what I saw."

"A lot of things in life don't make sense." Setting his cup back in the saucer, Adam raised his gaze to meet hers. "Any idea how long you'll be with us?"

Somehow *no bloody clue* didn't seem like an appropriate answer. "At least until I can pay for the repairs on my car." *And I know that it's safe for me to return to Dallas.*

"Which reminds me, why did you say the car wasn't yours?"

"Semantics."

"Excuse me?"

"I never wanted that car. I'm more of a practical-SUV kind of girl. Jonathan bought it for me, but, until the wedding day, I'd never even driven it."

"Ah. Sort of like the wife who gets a vacuum cleaner for a birthday gift."

"More like a new drill."

Adam laughed, a deep throaty rumble that made her want to laugh too. Even at the mess her ex had gotten her into. Her phone dinged a news alert, and she put down her cup to retrieve her cell from her pocket. *Jonathan Cox released on one-million-dollar bond.*

● ● ●

"Oh. My. God."

"What?" Becky dropped the egg chopper, poised to sprint over the table if Donna was in trouble.

"Look at this." Donna pointed to her laptop screen.

"A little hard to see from here." Next time she volunteered to bring appetizers to girls' night, she was bringing mini frozen quiches. Trying to cook deviled eggs with a pregnant woman on the sofa calling for her every two minutes was not a good plan.

"Well, get over here."

"Can't it wait?"

"No." Donna huffed.

"Okay." Hugging the bowl to her side, Becky grabbed a fork and decided she could mash cooked egg yolks from any room in the house. "What's so all-fired important?"

"This popped up on my home page."

Settling in on a corner of the sofa, Becky debated if she'd been called over because of the seventy-five-year-old woman who looked thirty-five, the before-and-after photos of a woman who had tried Dr. Oz's latest weight-loss fad or the two foods you should never eat. "I don't get it."

"Did you see what it says?"

"Don't eat bananas?"

"Not that." Donna jabbed her finger at the middle of the screen. "This. The article on Jonathan J. Cox."

"Why should I care about some crook out on bail?"

"This crook was arrested on his wedding day."

"Yeah. So?" Becky smashed eggs as she scanned the article.

"Look at the bride's name."

Becky read a little faster, and then she found it. *Holy crap.* "Do you think our Meg is Margaret Colleen O'Brien?"

"Sure sounds like it. I mean, how many women were getting married two weekends ago with the last name O'Brien who ran off in their wedding dress and haven't been seen since?"

"Does it say that?" Becky leaned closer.

"Skip to the end."

Her hands still, Becky straightened. "This also says her fiancé is wanted for swindling investors out of millions of dollars. You don't suppose she's an accomplice of some sort? A crook?" Tuckers Bluff wasn't exactly nirvana, but Becky didn't like the idea of a criminal duping the entire town into feeling sorry for her. And everyone had taken a liking to Meg rather quickly. Not something usual for small towns. Wasn't that what con artists were really, really good at?

"Why would someone, who helped steal millions of dollars, be hiding in Tuckers Bluff? I'd be on my way to Argentina."

"True." Maybe. This was all just a little too weird. "But if she gives us any investment advice, I'm calling D.J."

• • •

Waiting for Meg to come back downstairs from changing, Adam drank what must have been his hundredth cup of coffee.

"You'd better have a little something solid to chase that down with or you'll burn a hole in your stomach." Abbie slipped a piece of apple pie in front of him and slid into the other side of the booth.

"Hey, why don't you sit a spell?"

"Thanks." She winked at him. "I think I will."

Tuckers Bluff didn't have a local pub. This part of the county was dry as a bone, but, if someone sat around long enough nursing a beverage of choice, eventually Abbie would come around and lend an ear, much like a therapeutic bartender.

"It's nice that Becky and the girls invited Meg to join them tonight."

Adam nodded.

"If there's any chance of keeping her around, she's going to have to feel at home."

This time Adam skipped responding in any way. Ever since his fingertips had singed at the feel of Meg's soft skin, varied scenarios had been running rampant—of Meg in the kitchen, the living room, the dining room and his bed. His mind had already done a damn good job of making her feel at home. The problem was his mind also saw her smiling by the family Christmas tree, fawning over the ranch's bumper crop of springtime births and reading bedtime stories to children who suspiciously looked like him and her. Lust he could handle; thoughts of Margaret O'Brien, home and hearth were unfamiliar territory for him.

He should be keeping his distance. This wasn't her home. Home was the big city. But after a total of one family supper, two lengthy drives into town and brief daily stops to pick up takeout for himself and his staff—way more often than usual—without any effort on her part, Meg had gotten thoroughly and completely under his skin in a way he couldn't explain.

"What do you think?"

Adam hoped to hell that Abbie took his silence to mean he was considering her question, not wondering what on earth she'd said that he hadn't heard.

"I don't want to lose her, Adam. Not only has she caught on to the job faster than any greenhorn I've ever known, but the customers love her, and Frank could almost be described as pleasant."

Okay, that was interesting. Frank Carter—a career marine, a master gunnery sergeant—who ordered the wait staff around as though they were raw recruits in boot camp. He'd been called anything from surly and grumpy to silent and reserved, but *pleasant* never came close to describing Frank. "I honestly don't know what to say, Abbie."

"Well, you think on it. If anyone can figure out a way to keep her in town, you get my vote."

"Me?"

Footsteps bouncing down the back stairs announced Meg's impending arrival.

Abbie smiled and eased out of the seat. "Think about it."

He was still staring at Abbie's retreating back, contemplating if she knew something that he didn't, when Meg appeared by the table. "Ready whenever you are."

"All set." Adam stood up, grabbed his hat from its perch, then gestured for Meg to lead the way. His mind teetered back and forth from finding ways to do exactly as Abbie had asked—convincing Meg to stay in town—to accepting that she didn't belong at all. The truth was, no matter how captivating her smile or scintillating her laugh or enticing her bashful blush, Margaret O'Brien was still a mystery to unravel. In more ways than one.

CHAPTER THIRTEEN

It had taken a tremendous amount of willpower for Meg not to stay home and read through every updated news article on Jonathan. She'd quickly glanced through a couple, searching for any mention of her father. William O'Brien's name appeared as owner of BriteWay Investment Securities, LLC, whose involvement in criminal activities was still under investigation. From the sounds of it, every law enforcement agency from the SEC to the FBI had a hand in this case. According to the one article, several victims had already filed civil suits against Jonathan and her father's company. All of which meant things were going to take longer to blow over than she'd hoped.

Now here she stood, waiting for one of the sexiest men she'd ever laid eyes on to give her a ride to her first small-town girls' night out. What she couldn't decide was which made her more nervous, being in the cab of a pickup so close to Mr. Sex on a Stick or facing a houseful of women bound to ask a lot of questions which she wasn't prepared to answer. "Ready whenever you are."

"All set." Adam slid out of the booth and pushed to his feet. Large booted feet.

What was it they said about the size of a man's... *Don't go there, Meg.* When he gestured for her to go first, she hurried ahead. The last thing she needed was another long view of that jean-clad backside. She needed to wrap her mind around something more benign. Safe. "How far is Donna's?"

"Not very. I'll have you there in five minutes."

And why did her heart sink? Only five minutes was good. Better than good. Perfect. Alone with an almost honest-to-God Texas cowboy was not smart for a woman whose wedding and life had recently fallen apart like a damn house of cards. "Sounds good. Thanks again."

"Just being neighborly."

Neighborly. Right. Adam pulled open the door to the cab, and Meg grabbed the handle and hoisted herself up. Slamming down on the seat, she kept her gaze straight ahead. Adam Farraday was simply being neighborly, and she was behaving like a crushing teen. How pathetic was that?

"It's pretty fortunate for Abbie that you came along when you did. No one expected Donna to have to stop working so soon."

"That's what Abbie says. I'm glad I could help." And even more glad for the job. When she'd gotten in the Ferrari at the church, her only thought had been to get as far away from Dallas and the Jonathan mess as she could. The last thing her daddy needed was for her to tell the police or anyone else what she'd overheard.

"How are the special accounts coming along?" William O'Brien handed Jonathan a glass of after-dinner cognac.

"Excellent. I've got everything set up per your instructions. New investors are thrilled with the rate of return." Jonathan had taken a slow sip of what she knew would be a smooth, satisfying swallow.

"Good. Good. Looks like uniting the O'Briens and the Coxes will be very profitable for our growing family."

At the time Meg had been pleased that her Dad had trusted his soon-to-be son-in-law with anything special and profitable. But now it didn't look good for her father. She didn't believe for a minute that her daddy would steal from people who trusted him. But she'd already figured out that love had a way of blinding a person to the truth. She couldn't risk going home and being questioned. Men were sent to jail on lesser evidence than an overheard conversation by a daughter. She had to stay away.

"Have you given any thought to finding another place to stay?" Adam's words bled into her thoughts.

"Not really."

"There are a few empty houses available on the outskirts of

town. Some might go for a bargain now that oil prices are sinking like a newborn calf in a mud pit."

"I don't think I could afford a house."

"I could be speaking out of turn, but I'm guessing, if you asked, Abbie would clear out that little apartment and rent it to you cheap. Real cheap."

The place did have a lot of potential. But, if her luck was changing, by the time she paid off the repairs on her car, maybe it would be safe to go home. "I'll have to think about that."

A lazy smile eased the corners of his mouth upward. "Good. Good." The big truck had taken only a turn or two down a few long blocks when Adam slowed and pulled into the driveway. "Here we are."

A wooden house with a large front porch, holding the requisite pair of rocking chairs, reminded her of an era long gone. She glanced left then right, taking in the wall of shrubs, the clusters of recently planted spring flowers and the laughter floating her way through an open window. Add a little snow and blinking lights, and the home would have made the perfect Christmas card.

Her passenger door swung open, and Adam extended a hand. "Let me help you down."

A little more eagerly than she should have, Meg accepted the proffered hand and stepped from the truck. His hands found their way around her waist as he settled her to the ground. "Thank you."

"My pleasure." His eyes leveled with hers. For a few seconds, the way his gaze softened, shifting from her eyes to her mouth and back, she thought he was going to kiss her. Instead he took a step back, his hands falling heavily to his sides.

"There's a great new steak place in Butler Springs. I've been meaning to try it out."

Meg nodded.

"Would be nice if you'd join me."

"Yes," Meg mumbled.

"Tomorrow night?"

She nodded this time, her mouth suddenly dry and filled with cotton.

"Pick you up at six."

Her head bobbed again. Words stuck in her throat.

"Very well." He angled himself away from her and toward the front of the truck. "Guess I'll see you tomorrow at six."

"At six," she repeated, her gaze on Adam as he jogged around the hood and climbed into the truck. He'd slammed the door, started the engine, and, looking her way, his brows buckled into a deep frown. Concerned what might have gone wrong, it suddenly struck her that he was probably confused as to why she still stood rooted to the ground where he'd set her down. Taking a small step back, she waved nonchalantly as though he hadn't caught her mindlessly staring at him, then pivoted and hurried up the walk. Not until Becky opened the door and waved her in did Meg hear the rumble of the truck pulling away.

● ● ●

"So glad you could make it." A very pregnant woman Meg assumed was Donna waved from the sofa. "I've heard so much about you. Been dying to see who could take my place."

"No one," Becky said, heading to the kitchen. "Meg, what would you like to drink? We've got cola, diet Pepsi—"

"No aspartame now," someone she didn't recognize called from the opposite corner of the room.

"A nice pinot grigio," Becky continued without skipping a beat. "And a cabernet that Nora brought."

"And," Kelly added, "there's always a little frozen margarita mix in the fridge. I brought the tequila. Virgin margaritas and alcohol free wine for Donna."

Meg took a seat in the recliner closest to the TV. "A small glass of pinot would be nice."

"One white wine coming up." Becky nearly bounced into the kitchen. "And help yourself to anything on the table. I made the deviled eggs."

"Which means you could be taking your life into your own hands." Kelly laughed.

"I can cook," Becky snipped back.

For the next two hours the conversation went back and forth, much the same way from one friend to another. A lively debate ensued on whether to watch David Duchovny in *Return to Me* or Leonardo DiCaprio in *The Great Gatsby*, but Donna's vote counted double, since it was her house, and David's romantic comedy won. But the film in no way slowed the women's banter. By the time Duchovny rode up on a bicycle with the nun on the handlebars, the group of six women were laughing till they cried, Donna the only sober one in the bunch.

"Why don't things like that happen in real life?" Kelly sank lower on the sofa and leaned her head back, swirling a watered-down margarita in her hand.

"Probably"—Becky pushed to her feet—"because we don't live in Chicago."

"What does that have to do with it?" Donna asked, shifting in place.

"Except for the Farradays, we don't have very many Irishmen—or Italians—in west Texas."

"Only the Irish and Italians can be romantic?" Donna asked.

"Actually," Kelly chimed in, "the Irish and the Italians were the fun ones in the movie. David dear could have been a Texan."

"Texans can be fun," Nora slurred.

"They can dance," added a short blonde, sitting beside Kelly, whose name Meg had forgotten. "Both vertical and horizontal."

"Ooh," chorused throughout the room.

"Do tell." Kelly leaned forward. "Things have been so dry around here, I might turn to dust before a real man comes around."

The blonde flashed a saucy grin. "Now am I the kind of girl to kiss and tell?"

"Yes," everyone shouted back, and another burst of laughter erupted throughout the room.

"All I know is, if it was one of the Farradays, I may have to scratch your eyes out." Nora blew out a sigh. "Damn those men are prime grade-A beef."

Meg could almost feel the room swoon in agreement. Her fingers tightened on her nearly empty glass of wine, waiting for the name, mentally crossing her fingers that Adam hadn't been the one to recently do the horizontal tango with Blondie.

"Nah. Those boys won't mess with locals. If any of them dips their rig in a girl's oil well around here, you'd better be sure there'll be a wedding down the road."

Whatever else Blondie had to say about the ranch hand she'd gone two-stepping with last weekend took a backseat to her proclamation about impending nuptials. Surely she wasn't talking about a dinner date? Metaphorically speaking Blondie had to be referring to doing the deed. A one-night stand maybe. Not a dinner date? *Date*? Holy crap! She had a date with one of the men half the women in town wanted to sleep with.

"What about you, Meg?" Donna asked.

"Me?" She did her best to put on a casual smile that said, *I have nothing to hide*. "Not much action here either."

"But you were getting married?" Nora immediately slapped both her hands over her mouth. "Oops. We weren't supposed to say anything."

"We?" Meg asked.

All eyes in the room developed a sudden interest in the floor. Becky was the first to look Meg in the face. "It's no secret you came into town wearing a wedding dress, and today in the—"

"News." Meg's shoulders sagged.

"Yeah." Becky shrugged. "We agreed not to mention anything in the article."

"I see." Meg lifted her glass to the light. Not enough wine in the world would make her story any prettier. "Thought I'd met my knight in shining armor. Half an hour before I was supposed to walk down the aisle, I discovered he wasn't quite the man I thought him to be. Turns out the suit of armor was pretty rusty, and the knight was nothing more than a sleazebag." She downed the last of the wine in a single swallow. "Yep. Total sleazebag."

"Ouch." Becky winced.

Blondie pointed at Meg. "You know what they say about falling off a horse."

Everyone in the room nodded, but Kelly was the one grinning like the Cheshire cat. "You have to get right back on."

"Exactly," Blondie asserted. And again all heads in the room nodded in agreement. Of course with the amount of liquor that had been consumed, Blondie could have suggested streaking down Main Street, and all the ladies would probably have roared in agreement.

"Here's to saving a horse and riding a cowboy!" Kelly raised her glass. "Welcome to Tuckers Bluff, Meg O'Brien. I think you're gonna fit in just fine."

Meg raised her glass with her new friends and, for a heated moment, thought if only it were that easy.

CHAPTER FOURTEEN

Pinching the bridge of his nose, Adam dialed his brother D.J. and willed the tension headache building from his shoulders to his eyeballs to go away. Usually he only worked half days on Saturday, but today the patients kept coming. On his feet all day with back-to-back surgeries, every muscle longed for a long hot shower.

On the other end of the line D.J.'s cell stopped ringing. "Farraday."

"You sound like your day is going the same as mine."

"I've had better, if that's what you mean."

"Yeah. That's what I mean. Any word on the dog?" Last night D.J. had mentioned making rounds to neighboring ranches on the frills of his jurisdiction, and Adam had convinced him to add investigating a lost or missing dog to his schedule.

"Nada. No one is missing a dog—stray, working, or otherwise—and no signs of buzzards over a dead animal."

"Thanks." That was pretty much what Adam had expected to hear, but still he was hoping for more definitive answer. "See ya tomorrow?"

"Yeah. Listen." D.J. paused. "About Meg."

"What about her?"

"How well do you know her?"

"About as well as you do. Why?" D.J.'s muffled scoff surprised him. "What aren't you telling me?"

This time a heavy sigh drifted through the airways. "Nothing, but be careful."

"You're not making sense." And Adam was way too tired for this game of cop and mouse.

"Never mind. Just don't do anything I wouldn't do." The click of another call coming in sounded in Adam's ear. "That's the office. Have to go."

What the hell was that all about?

"Did you get a hold of D.J.?" Becky Wilson stood in the doorway to Adam's office.

"Just hung up."

"Any word on the dog?"

He repeated what D.J. had told him, but his mind was still struggling with D.J.'s cryptic comments about Meg.

Becky shrugged. "Let's hope that's a good thing. Maybe you and Meg were just hallucinating."

"That'll be a first. Simultaneous and consistent mirages."

"Makes about as much sense as anything else." Smiling, Becky pushed away from the door. "I haven't seen you eat anything today. Have you?"

"I grabbed a yogurt after the yellow Lab's surgery."

"That's not a meal. Want to head over for an early supper at the café?"

"Not tonight. I have other plans." Plans he was very much looking forward to and had no intention of letting his hypercautious brother spoil.

"Plans?" Becky's brows arched high on her forehead.

"Yes, Miss Wilson." He pushed to his feet. "And if it meets with your approval, ma'am, I'm calling it a day and see if I can't shower out some of these kinks."

Grinning like the giddy teen he so fondly remembered, she rolled her eyes and shook her head at him. "News flash. There are much better ways to relieve tension. You should give it some thought." Before he could lob a reply, Becky paused, hanging on the doorjamb, and added, "And, for what it's worth, Meg's really nice."

Like a shot she was gone down the corridor. He had to give the kid points; she was right about relieving stress. It had been way too long since he'd been with a woman. Too bad he couldn't do anything about it with Meg. All the Farraday brothers had one unbreakable rule: they didn't screw around with friends. And since most people living in Tuckers Bluff had been born and raised here, just about every single woman within a fifty-mile radius was in some way, shape or form a friend.

While dating a gal from the next town or two over wasn't always convenient, it certainly made breaking up much easier. In a town this small, there was no avoiding anyone. A relationship gone bad could be a nightmare run-in at the café, gas station or grocery store. No. Even Meg would have to be off intimate limits. And, if he repeated that to himself nonstop for the next hour and a half, maybe he'd believe it.

• • •

Meg spun in front of the closet door mirror. She'd hated to use credit with the sisters, but there simply wasn't enough money in the coffers for a new dress otherwise. Since there was no way in hell she was going to dinner in Butler Springs wearing her work clothes, credit with the sisters had been her only option.

Meg had gravitated toward a simple tan sheath dress. Every girl needed something in her closet that could be dressed up with a string of pearls or dressed down with a pair of sandals. Since Meg had neither sandals nor pearls, practical for tonight made no sense. Instead she'd gone with Sister's suggestion and bought the dark blue sleeveless with the belted waist and flared skirt and a lightweight black sweater for later. Sister had been right. Staring into the mirror, Meg had to resist the urge to twirl around the way she and her friends had done when they were young girls.

Tonight's outfit consisted of her new dress, with new accessories—neutral-colored shoes and a matching small purse. The shoes were almost as striking as the dress. Pointed toe with a narrow heel, not too high, not too low, and a diagonal strap across her arch, the shoes made a classic statement. For a couple of country women out in the middle of nowhere in west Texas, the sisters had a fabulous small selection of women's attire. No matter what Meg needed, the sisters always seemed to have the perfect piece in just the right size.

A rap at the front door stopped her playful swirling. Straightening her shoulders and smoothing down the flowing material for no reason other than to calm her nerves, Meg maneuvered the obstacle course to the front door. Sucking in one last breath, she yanked it open. Gracefully. "Hi."

Adam tipped his hat at her, and appreciation shone in his eyes. "Hi."

It would have been too easy to stand here all night lost in depths of eyes as blue as the Mediterranean, but Meg had made enough of a fool of herself with Jonathan for several women's lifetimes. Forcing herself to look away, she waved toward the only two chairs in the room not piled high with boxes. Unable to sleep, she'd spent last night moving boxes and cleaning off the space. "Come in."

Looking over her shoulder, he rocked on his heels and cast a quick glance around the compact space. "Thanks, but I made reservations."

"Oh." Jumping back, she nodded. "Let me get my purse and we can leave."

"Also"—he cleared his throat and stretched out his right arm. "I brought these. It's not much but …"

"Flowers." Her word came out soft as a breath.

"The only place I could find blue flowers on short notice was in Mrs. Peabody's yard. I had to promise her free vet care for six months in exchange for letting me cut her prize hydrangeas."

"That was very sweet of you. It will only take a minute to put them in water." She opened the door a little wider for him to wait inside and hurried to the tiny wall of cabinets that passed for a kitchen and sink. "These are beautiful."

Opening and closing several cabinet doors, she finally found a suitable vase. It had been so long since Jonathan had given her flowers. Long-stem roses delivered by a florist. At the time she'd been delighted with the gorgeous arrangement. Now they couldn't compare to the effort it had taken Adam to coerce a neighbor into parting with her prized blooms. *Blue*. Meg's favorite color. *He remembered*. Was he this thoughtful about everything?

Her mind circled back to that first morning when he'd insisted on putting her in his truck so she wouldn't break an ankle. How he'd gone off in search of a potentially wounded animal even though he was bone-tired from having been up all night with a mama horse in trouble. From all appearances, Adam was the sort of man who women's dreams were made of. Then again, Meg had learned a lesson the hard way about falling for appearances. Placing the vase on the small entry table by the door, Meg studied her date for the night. Her gut said Adam Farraday was everything he appeared to be, and—if that were true—that mama horse wasn't the only one in big trouble.

• • •

This was absolutely ridiculous. Adam felt like a teen on his first date. Bringing her hand-picked flowers. Way to show his country roots.

"Is something wrong?"

"No. Sorry, just thinking too much."

"I know how that is." At ease now, she relaxed into the seat. "My mind loves going round and round in circles. Kicking around the same thought over and over. Twisting and turning events, seeking out every possible outcome."

"Life is unpredictable." After all, how many people expect to stumble across a beautiful woman on a lonely stretch of highway?

"Preaching to the choir." Meg lifted her head and swiveled in her seat. "Have you ever been married?"

He shook his head.

"Engaged?"

Though he and his high school sweetheart had talked marriage from time to time, there'd never even been a promise ring, and it had all ended when he'd gone off to college. He shook his head again.

"In love?"

"No one gets out of junior high without thinking they've been in love at least once."

"I don't mean lust. I mean love."

He knew what she meant. He'd come close a few times. "Not the way you mean."

Her brows shot up high on her forehead.

"I dated a girl pretty steady back in college. Our senior year as graduation approached we had to make a choice. Either she'd stay in College Station with me while I went through vet school, or we'd go our separate ways and move on with our lives. I loved Connie. And she loved me. Maybe if we'd decided to stay together, it would have grown into the stable kind of love that leaves you contented in your old age."

"But you didn't give it a chance?"

"I would have. At the time I thought it was right, but Connie knew we would only be moving forward with an engagement because it was expected of us. She wanted something more." He'd never actually said that out loud, not even to himself. "Something that I couldn't give her."

"Maybe if I'd have been as smart as Connie, I wouldn't be in this mess."

"What mess are you in, Meg?" There, he'd come right out and asked her.

Sucking her lips in between her teeth, she closed her eyes for a moment, before sitting tall again and looking straight at him. "It's no secret. Not anymore. My fiancé is a crook. A swindler. He used my father's company to pull in investors, promised them ridiculous returns, and, rather than invest their money, he'd used the newest dupes to pay 'dividends' to the previous investors."

"A Ponzi scheme." For the last few years blood-sucking scam artists like her ex seemed to be breeding like greedy rabbits.

"Yeah, that's what the FBI told me."

"FBI?"

Her eyes closed, and her head fell against the backrest. "The wedding was only thirty minutes away. I was in the Ready Room. Probably the first bride in the history of weddings to arrive early. There was a bit of a commotion outside my door. My maid of honor's husband was arguing with a guy who had a badge pinned to his belt. I'm not even sure why I noticed the badge." She turned to face Adam again. "Jonathan didn't have any close friends. He asked my maid of honor's husband to be his best man. Made a joke that my friends were his friends, but I should have seen there was something more to it."

"A lot of people are shy or introverted or too highly focused on education or a career to maintain a friendship. Most people don't jump to the conclusion that this means they're crooks or swindlers."

"No." She chuckled. "I guess not. But still …"

He waited a long beat before prodding her to continue. "What happened next?"

"The FBI agent apologized for breaking up the wedding. Something about delayed warrants, freezing assets, and it couldn't be helped. Now that I think back, I'm pretty sure, before I opened the door, he'd argued with my maid of honor's husband that, if I wasn't involved, I'd be thanking them for not waiting for the honeymoon to arrest Jonathan." She chuckled again. Not an amused sound but more of a caustic huff. "That would have been hard to accomplish. We were supposed to go to Paris."

"I'm guessing you mean France. Not Texas."

This time her laugh was softer, almost musical. "Not Texas."

This wasn't quite the "caught her ex banging the best friend" scenario he'd expected to hear. But at least it wasn't the "legally married to a dangerous man" case that he'd feared either. "And that's when you got in your car and kept driving."

"I don't think I've ever been so angry in my life."

Anger made sense. The first stage of grieving.

"If he were here now, I still think I'd shoot his balls off."

Adam felt his own constrict in his boxers. "A little drastic, don't you think?"

"No. Apparently the money he was stealing from my father's clients wasn't enough for him. He pretty much wiped out all my accounts too. And maxed my credit cards."

"What about work? You must have a job in Dallas."

"*Had*. After the wedding I was going to focus on my own business."

"What's that?"

"I'm in hotel management. Dallas has the perfect demographics for boutique hotels. Jonathan was handling the finances, and I would handle the hotel details."

"And now that's gone."

Her head bobbed, and water pooled in her eyes. A tear escaped down her cheek, and she swiped at it with the back of her hand.

"I'm sorry." The words were pretty lame, but it was all he could do.

"Some date I'm turning out to be." She wiped one more time and plastered on a shaky smile.

"I could say the same. I'm the idiot who asked you to go over all this. I really am sorry he hurt you." Adam was a little surprised just how much he wanted to get his hands on her ex. And break him into little pieces.

"Well, the FBI guy was right about one thing. I'm very glad they didn't wait." She shifted around again, her knee resting on the seat. "Turns out I was in love with a mirage. With the idea of being in love. Every girl dreams of Prince Charming and her wedding day. I should be more upset."

He didn't want to point out that she looked pretty upset to him.

"Not about the wedding or the money or what he did to my fath … family. *That* I'm mad as hell about. But I'm not even a little disappointed that I'm not married to Jonathan. It's rather frightening to realize I could know so little about love."

On the edge of town in Butler Springs, the lights from the

new steakhouse appeared ahead. Adam eased off the gas and turned into the parking lot. So much had been shared during the drive that his head was swimming. Trotting around to the passenger side, he opened the door and helped her down, as was his habit now. Only this time close enough to get a whiff of her shampoo. Something sweet and vanilla.

"Thank you." She smiled, the sadness in her eyes gone. "Again."

"You're welcome. Again." He lingered a little longer than he should have. Long enough to notice the flash of heat in her eyes, sending all the blood in his veins south. Forcing himself to ease back, Adam wondered just how much of a hold Meg's ex fiancé had on her.

CHAPTER FIFTEEN

"I don't believe it." Meg shook her head, failing miserably at holding back her laughter. "You seriously tied your sister to the goal posts?"

"Guilty as charged. But in our defense she was in full protective gear. When Grace complained to Aunt Eileen, she refused to believe we would do anything so obnoxious."

"You got away with it?" Her voice went up a few octaves.

"Nope." Adam slid his wallet from his back pocket. "Finn tattled. Though not on purpose. He told Aunt Eileen how he wanted a real hockey stick for Christmas. That struck her as odd, so she asked him if he liked playing hockey with his brothers. Finn being the youngest boy didn't get to play with Connor, Brooks, and me very often so he was all excited that we'd let him on the team."

"One team?"

"With only six of us, you play keep away. Alternating time periods. One team tries to score, the other team keeps the puck away. Three on one team. Three on the other."

"And that's why you needed a seventh for goalkeeper."

"Exactly." He placed several bills inside the black folder with the dinner tab. "Then Aunt Eileen hit him with the trick question."

Meg couldn't stop from smiling. The more stories she heard, the more she really liked Adam's aunt. His whole family for that matter. "What was it?"

"Bet it's no fun having to play with a girl?"

"Oh, boy. He fell for it, didn't he?"

"He was only seven. Yeah. He fell for it. That night, after supper, my father sat the six of us down in the library and asked us outright."

"What did you say?"

"The truth. None of us were ever willing to lie to Dad. We might skirt the truth from time to time. Leave out a few facts. Maybe drop chaff and distract him but never lied to his face."

"None of you?"

Adam pushed to his feet and reaching her seat, pulled out her chair for her. "None of us. Ever."

"Not even to save your own skins?" She almost jumped in place when his warm hand settled at the small of her back, steering her toward the door.

"If you can't trust a man's word, you can't trust the man."

The way Adam's fingers barely rested against her back kept Meg from thinking clearly. Thoughts were taking twice as long to travel from her brain to her mouth and then form words. "Trust. Yes."

"A man is nothing without respect. Honor is important in our family, more than lip service."

There was no doubt that, unlike her sniveling ex, honor and respect were tattooed on the Farraday DNA. "Which is why one of your brothers is a marine."

"Three actually."

"Three?"

"Once a marine always a marine. Connor and D.J. both did four years each."

"Let me guess. D.J. was military police?"

Nodding, Adam pushed open the exit door, cast a quick glance up and down the street. "It's a beautiful evening. There's a park with a small pond at the other end of the street. Would you like to take a walk?"

"Yes. I feel like a turkey at Thanksgiving. I could use the exercise. It was, by the way, incredibly delicious. Thank you."

"My pleasure." He tipped his hat and extended his elbow to her.

All she needed was a gingham dress and a straw bonnet to feel like a character in an old TV Western. For a few seconds she let herself bask in the serenity of the moment.

"What about your other brothers? Did either of them consider the military?"

"Not really. Didn't seem practical for Brooks or me, both of us looking at eight years of education plus four more years of internship and residency. Finn has been married to the ranch since before puberty." Adam chuckled under his breath. "The kid was grown up and ready to take charge by his tenth birthday."

Duty to family was as obvious to any observer of this tight-knit clan as the west Texas horizon, but apparently duty to country was equally strong in the Farraday family. And, if the brothers she had yet to meet were anything like Adam, she could probably add duty to strangers to the list. "How long has Ethan been in?"

The muscle in Adam's jaw pulled taut before he opened his mouth to speak. "Going on seven years. He'll do his twenty, or however long Uncle Sam lets him fly."

He drew quiet for a second, and, even not having anyone close in the military, Meg knew what had just run through Adam's mind. *Or as long the enemy doesn't shoot him down.*

"Don't get me wrong," he continued. "Ethan loves the ranch just as much as the rest of us, but he loves flying that helicopter more than ten ranches or one hundred women."

"Fond of women, is he?" Lowering her chin while gazing up at him, she gave her best effort at shooting him a coy grin.

"Well …" His words trailed off. Through his jacket, she could feel the strong muscles in his arm bunching with tension.

"It's okay." She chuckled. "I was teasing. I've never been a soldier, or a man, but I'm sure there's a marine equivalent to a girl in every port. Maybe several. Girls. Not ports."

"Men who work hard tend to play hard." Adam didn't look at her. He kept his gaze on the sidewalk ahead. "We read all the hype about the SEAL teams or Special Forces, and imagine all the things about the black ops no one tells us, but teams don't get where they're going without help."

"Helicopter pilots," she mumbled. A distant memory of a

news story on the Chinook helicopter crash during the secret mission that killed Osama Bin Laden scrambled forward in her mind. For the first time since hearing bits and pieces about the remaining Farraday brothers, Meg realized just how dangerous a world Ethan Farraday lived in.

"Here we are." Adam stopped at the edge of the park. "What do you think?"

"It's like stepping back in time." A lush green lawn, surrounded by cobblestone pathways and newly blooming beds, all focused around the yellow and white Victorian bandstand dead center.

"They hold fairs and festivals here throughout the year." Letting his hand fall, he once again brought it to rest on the small of her back and directed her up the steps.

On the other side of the lone gingerbread-like structure, a small pond shimmered with reflected moonlight. "Wish I had a camera. My little phone takes terrible pictures."

From his breast pocket, Adam pulled out his smart phone. "Here you go. It's better than most cameras."

What was it about his smile that made her heart dance and her mouth go dry? "Thank you." Turning her back to him, she had to suck in a deep breath when he came to stand behind her and rested his hands on her shoulders.

Why did he have to keep touching her? Not that there was anything rude or untoward about the friendly gesture, but her lungs had seized, and her hands were nearly trembling with the need to lay her fingertips on him. Anywhere. Everywhere.

Get a grip, Margaret Colleen.

Falling for a pretty face had already gotten Meg into enough trouble. She raised the camera and snapped a photograph of the sparkling water. Another of the moon high in the sky. She took a chance and flipped the lens and saw that Adam was looking ahead over her shoulder to some distant point. She snapped a photo of him. And another. Turning slightly to the right, she snapped a shot of a mama duck, waddling away from the pond with a row of ducklings behind her. Before she could click on the next shot, Adam leaned down, his lips against her ear, and all sorts of tingly sensations began ricocheting inside her.

"Let me know if you start to feel a chill."

Chill? Was he kidding? If she got any warmer, she'd self-combust. Had she ever in her entire life been so turned on by a man's hands on her fully clothed shoulders? By the sound of his smooth-as-aged-brandy voice in her ear? Would he totally freak out if she whirled around and kissed him until she'd swallowed him whole?

God she needed to reel in her emotions. Taking in long shallow breaths, she captured, or at least pretended to capture, a few more photos. Not wanting to lose the connection of his hands on her and yet not sure she could utter an intelligible sentence, she glanced down to text the photos to herself. Her throwaway phone meant she could receive the photos unnoticed. At least she hoped the hell so. And, if she was wrong, at this moment, she didn't give a rat's ass. All she wanted was to have the photograph of that strong chiseled face to remind her on cold and lonely nights that there are places in this world where good men really do exist.

● ● ●

Why was he torturing himself? With every breath he could smell the scent of her shampoo. That same vanilla he'd noticed earlier at the café. Only this time it was mixed with a floral blend of some mild perfume. A scent that had him almost on his knees with wanting her. Or maybe it wasn't the perfume at all. Just her. The way she covered her mouth when she was trying not to laugh. The way her eyes lit up at the sight of the duck and her ducklings. How she took his picture when she thought he wasn't looking.

Lord, he wanted this woman. But no matter how much she insisted her ex-fiancé and the canceled wedding of only a couple of weeks ago were far behind her, a thing of the past, his gut told him that he was dealing with a filly who could easily spook if he moved too fast. And right now he wanted fast and hard, and then to do it all over again easy and slow.

Beneath his fingers her shoulders trembled, and he didn't dare think it was because of him. This early in the season the evening air was still crisp. Cool. "We should head back to the car."

"Just another minute." Her hands moved quickly. "Last ... photo ... sent." Sporting a triumphant smile, she spun around to face him. "All ..." Dark hungry eyes settled on his lips. Then slowly, tipping her head back, her gaze lifted and leveled with his. "All. Done."

His phone clutched in one hand, her other hand splayed flat on his chest. A spark of surprise flickered in her slate-blue orbs. Had she felt his racing heart stampeding beneath her fingertips? Or was she merely responding to the hunger in his eyes? Or maybe it was the proof of how much he wanted her, stiffly pressing between them, the not-so-hidden elephant on the gazebo.

Whatever the reason, he had two choices. Take a deep breath, step back, put some distance between them, then return Meg safely to the café. But his second option held a great deal more appeal. Sliding his hands down her side in a gentle caress, his arms eased behind her back, settling low on her spine, pressing her even closer against him as his head lowered, never breaking eye contact until the second his lips touched hers. Everything about her fit perfectly, molded to him, blended with him, captured him. Fire burned from within, and Meg O'Brien was his only hope of quenching the flames. Tongues tangled and collided; hands roamed and explored. When she released the tiniest moan of pleasure, Adam almost lost what little control he still had; his hips rocked toward her in a dance as old as the ages.

Just one more taste. One more caress. One more second of her body pressing against his. And more than anything else at this very moment, he knew one more of anything with Meg O'Brien would not be enough.

CHAPTER SIXTEEN

What the hell was she doing? Meg was in the midst of the best damn kiss she'd ever had in her entire life— better even than most of the sex she'd ever had in her entire life. That's what the hell she was doing. And she damn well didn't want to stop.

This man knew what he was doing; his hands barely moved, and yet the lightest of strokes had a rush of heat shooting to every nerve ending. Lord, this man could kiss. She felt the pull of need between her legs with every curl of his tongue.

"Meg"—Adam breathed against her mouth—"we're in public." He kissed her lips, the edge of her mouth, down to her chin and back to the opposite corner, before pulling away. Keeping her close, his hands still on her hips, he let his chin come to rest atop her head. Slow ragged breaths mirrored her own attempt to gather her wits and get her body under control. "You have no idea how much I really hate to say this, but we need to slow down."

Common sense would agree with him. Except at this moment hers was nowhere to be found. Taking in a long calming breath and releasing it in a slow stuttered huff, she rested her forehead against Adam's chest. The rapid tattoo of his heartbeat matched hers. He was right of course. They weren't a couple of kids making out on Lover's Lane. He was a grown man and, stopping like this, public or not, had to be as hard on him as it was on her.

"We wouldn't want the neighbors calling the police on us."

"That would be D.J.?" she mumbled into his shirt.

"No. But he'd find out."

She almost laughed. "Gotta love brothers."

"Especially the one who would know I was arrested for public indecency."

That was debatable. As far as she was concerned, Adam Farraday was way more than decent. "I guess." She straightened in the circle of his arms, and almost whimpered when he let go of her and took a half step in retreat. "I guess we should head back to Tuckers Bluff."

"Yeah."

In simultaneous moves that could have been choreographed, their heads dipped and each took two steps back and, more specifically, apart. In an easy silence, they doubled back to the parking lot. In full gentleman mode, Adam opened the truck's door for her and waited till she was comfortably seated to trot around to the driver's side and start his pickup.

Out of town and on the straight stretch of empty road, a contented smile tugged at the corners of her mouth. "That was nice."

Adam's stony expression softened.

She could see the tension roll off his shoulders. "Very nice."

A few minutes out of town, he reached across the console and hooked a few fingers with hers. By the time they were halfway home, their hands were entwined in a comfortable clasp, and the conversation had shifted to scattered stories of growing-up-city versus growing-up-country. Not once did either broach the subjects of her failed wedding day, her lousy judgment in character, men, or how long she would be staying in town and, more important, why was she staying.

• • •

So many questions teased at the tip of his tongue. And yet he didn't attempt to find answers. Not now. Not tonight. Right now his only concern was getting himself under control and them back to Tuckers Bluff. The way he felt at the moment, he wasn't sure an ice-cube bath could dampen his libido. In his mind he was already running through a variety of ways to extend their time together. Coffee at the café seemed the safest. Any suggestion that involved his place or hers, and he couldn't promise he'd be able to keep his hands, or anything else, off of her. Despite the burning kiss they'd shared in the park, he wasn't convinced she was really ready to handle much more.

His simple plan for late-night coffee and companionship came crashing down as he drove into town and realized the hour. The café was dark. He bit down on his back teeth and accepted the fact that Abbie's early night had sealed the deal on this evening ending sooner than later. Easing down the street, a futile attempt to prolong his time with Meg, Adam finally pulled into the lot and parked by the back entrance to her upstairs apartment. Without saying a word, he hopped out and hurried to the passenger side. "Safely home, my lady."

Meg giggled, and he realized how much he liked the sound. And wanted to hear it again. Revisiting his debate over inviting her inside, he spotted the black and white police car ambling up the street. When the car stopped at the curb, Adam's spine straightened him to his full height.

"What's the matter?" Meg turned her head, looking over her shoulder, and followed his gaze. He knew the second she spotted D.J. getting out of his patrol car. Her shoulders stiffened, and her grip on his hand tightened almost imperceptibly. The nervous tension rolled off her in stifling waves.

Neither of them said a word, waiting for D.J. to spot them standing in the back of the lot. It took only a few seconds for the chief of police to see Adam's truck and a few more to focus on the two of them beside it. When D.J. moved forward to cross the street, Meg took a small step closer to Adam.

The gesture almost made him smile. He liked that she instinctively moved closer to him for protection. He liked it a lot. "What brings you here, little brother?"

The same height as his brother, Adam knew D.J. didn't take kindly to being referred to as *little* anything, but Adam could see in the tic of D.J.'s jaw that whatever brought him here would not be joked away. He came to a stop in front of them.

"Evening." D.J. tipped his hat at Meg. "Could we go inside for a few minutes? I need to speak with you."

Meg seemed to hesitate, like she was going to say no, then her eyes looked up to the second floor. "I'm not set up for company."

Having seen the place earlier this evening, Adam knew the only thing the apartment was set up for was warehouse storage.

"I'm afraid this is official." His gaze cut to Adam.

If D.J. thought Adam was going to leave Meg alone to face D.J. in his official capacity, he had another think coming. "Why don't we do this across the street? My furniture's easy to get to."

Meg turned a thankful gaze in his direction.

"I think you know what this is about." D.J. kept his attention on her, ignoring his brother. "It's up to you, Meg."

She nodded, and, without a word, the three crossed the street in almost military parade fashion. Left, right; left, right. With every step Adam's stomach coiled like a rattler about to strike. Before D.J. showed up, Adam wouldn't have dared touch Meg again. Not unless they planned to share breakfast. But now, concern for her had his balls shriveling and his arm winding protectively around her waist. He'd seen that look on his brother's face before. And, if the past was any indication, tonight was not going to end well for Meg.

• • •

Meg wanted to believe this upcoming tête-à-tête was nothing for her to worry about, but hairs bristling on the back of her neck told her otherwise. In eerie silence they crossed the street and, one by one, filed into Adam's apartment.

Inside was not what she'd expected. Slowly crossing the threshold, she took her time looking around. Large leather furniture graced the living room—that much wasn't out of the ordinary for a single man, nor the dark wood pub table and chairs claiming the dining area. But it was the updated kitchen with espresso-colored cabinets and marble-looking countertops that really caught her by surprise. The gadgets along the counter implied someone with an interest in cooking. The walls displayed tasteful framed photographs. Beautiful artwork and the occasional knickknack graced the tables and shelves, and gave the place a very manly, yet homey feel. Somehow she'd expected an antiquated apartment, much like the café rooms she currently occupied with sparse leftover college furniture.

Adam led the way to the sofa. He didn't bother with polite offerings of food or drink, and Meg wrapped her thoughts around the possible reasons D.J. would want to talk to her officially. She was the first to sit. Adam took the spot beside her, and D.J. sat in the chair facing them.

"What's this all about, D.J.?" Adam kept his voice low and even. Something she wasn't sure she could have done.

Adam may have been the one to ask the question, but it was Meg that D.J. responded to. "I'm sure you've already heard about your ex-fiancé making bail."

Meg nodded. "It was all over the news last night."

"What you don't know is that he's offering to make a deal in exchange for turning state's evidence against your father."

"No." The single syllable sounded more like a cry than a denial.

His hand already between them, Adam shifted in place and folded Meg's palm into his. "And you know this how?"

D.J. shook his head the slightest bit. "You really need to put a little more faith in me."

"And you really need to answer my question. How do you know?"

"I still have friends in Dallas. Connections." He must have seen the confusion on Meg's face because he quickly continued, "After I separated from the Marine Corps I was with Dallas P.D."

Meg nodded, not sure how any of this was about to impact her.

D.J.'s severe expression softened slightly. "Meg, I'm sorry, but the grand jury indicted your father today. Securities fraud."

Fear for her father stuck in her throat.

"It gets worse."

Worse? How could it be worse?

D.J. leaned forward. "You've been labeled a person of interest."

"Me?"

"It looks like Jonathan is pointing fingers at everyone. There have been some questionable expend—"

"That son of a bitch." Meg shot up out of her seat. "That lying, cheating"—her hands fisted at her side—"bastard!"

There was no missing the look the two brothers exchanged.

"What?" She looked to D.J. "What aren't you telling me?"

"I can't ignore that you're here in Tuckers Bluff," D.J. answered. "The FBI is sending two agents as we speak. I'm supposed to keep you in custody."

"Surely that won't be necessary." Adam stood and, placing himself at her back, let his hands fall on her shoulders. "She's not going to run."

"She did before."

"It's not what you think," she mumbled.

"Why don't you tell me what I think?" D.J. said sternly. "And don't leave anything out."

CHAPTER SEVENTEEN

A dam sat quietly as Meg recounted everything from the FBI in the church hall before the wedding to how she found herself on the road to town.

Fingers twisting together, she seemed to grow more concerned discussing her father.

"How does this work now? Is he going to jail?"

"The police will be arresting him based on the indictment. He'll face the judge and request bail. Whether or not it's granted, or for how much, depends on a lot of things. I'm not a lawyer or a judge."

"She needs a lawyer." Adam knew of a few good attorneys in the county. The ones who wrote up wills and settled minor disputes. But none that he'd trust with Meg's future. "You must know someone?" Adam said to his brother.

D.J.'s eyes dimmed into narrow slits as he studied Adam. He wasn't wondering anything different than Adam was. Adam had known Margaret Colleen O'Brien for only two weeks and had had all of one official date with her, and yet he was ready to step up on her behalf. If D.J. asked Adam why, he wouldn't be able to answer, but he knew in his gut he couldn't do anything else. This was about more than a raging hard-on for a woman who could bring him to his knees with just a kiss. Maybe it was the way she worried about an injured dog the first time he'd seen her. Or how she scrambled to do a job she'd never been trained for her first day at the café. Or the way she'd agreed to play cards with his aunt, the only woman who—until now—had ever mattered to him.

"Adam—"

"Do you know someone?" Adam repeated.

"Excuse me." Meg looked from one brother to the other. "I

know a lawyer."

The simple fact that she didn't protest needing an attorney to be questioned by the FBI told him there was more she hadn't told him. But Adam refused to believe she was a swindler. That made no sense at all. Not only because there was no reason for her to run off and lick her wounds if she'd been privy to her ex-fiancé's shenanigans but because of the way she behaved around him and everyone else in this town.

"At this time the FBI just want to question you, but Adam is right. It never hurts to have a good lawyer at your side."

She lowered her head and pulled out her phone. Adam watched her long slim fingers slide across the screen, scroll and tap. Phone to her ear, everyone waited. "Hi, Mom. Yes. I'm okay. No, I'm not ready to come home." She glanced up at D.J. "Mom, I think I need a lawyer."

Of all the ways he could have predicted this evening would end, having Meg awaiting interrogation by the FBI was most definitely not one of them. Dragging his attention away from Meg and the way she tightly held the phone at her ear, Adam looked to his brother.

Leaning forward, hands clasped loosely between his knees, D.J. was the portrayal of a casual observer, but Adam knew his brother to be anything but. D.J. was on alert, listening carefully, and Adam suspected by the tic in his jaw, allowing Meg to chat with her mother was not typical protocol.

As a matter of fact, Adam suspected none of what had just gone down in his living room were standard operating procedures. Most likely, had Meg been anyone else, a stranger the town had not taken in as one of their own, this conversation would have taken place in D.J.'s office at the station. Possibly behind bars. That wasn't a thought Adam wanted to dwell on. Every prison movie he'd ever seen flashed in front of him at high speed. The idea of Meg behind bars for even an hour, never mind years, made him want to puke. And he had a cast-iron stomach.

"I know, Mom. I'm sorry I worried you." Meg's words pulled

Adam's attention back to her. He could only imagine what his family would go through if one of them disappeared without a word.

Meg turned and rummaged through her purse, retrieving a pen and paper. "Shoot."

D.J.'s gaze remained trained on Meg. Did he really think she would try something sneaky? Speak in code? Give away classified information? Or maybe overpower them both and escape?

For Adam the worst part was feeling totally helpless. All of his life the Farradays had lived by the creed "where there's a will, there's a way." His father had pushed them all to follow their dreams, no matter the challenges. Nothing that couldn't be accomplished with a little elbow grease and brain power. Except fixing this.

Shifting his attention from Meg to his brother, a pop of light caught his eye. Looking out the window, he searched for the source. The only light on the street at this hour was the sign for the Silver Spurs Café. Outside his window there was nothing but the pitch of night, and then there it was again. Another pop, only this time it drew a line before disappearing.

"What is it?" D.J. asked, his eyes following Adam's.

"I don't know."

Seconds ticked by, and Adam wondered if this would be another one of those inexplicable incidents, like the dog. And there it was again.

He and D.J. jumped to their feet and spun around at Meg.

"Hang up," D.J. ordered.

Meg's eyes grew white rimmed with surprise.

"Now."

"Uh, I have to go, Mom. I'll call soon. I promise." She swiped at the phone, and eyes filled with fear turned to Adam.

"Are you expecting anyone at your place?" Adam asked.

Meg shook her head.

Adam and D.J. locked gazes, and D.J.'s chin dipped a fraction in agreement. Someone was prowling inside Meg's place with a flashlight, and they needed to get to him before he got to Meg.

D.J. unsnapped his holster and swung around to Meg. "You stay put. Do not move. Do not make any calls. And stay away from the window."

"But—"

"Stay," Adam added, already halfway to the door behind his brother.

Butler County wasn't immune to crime. Especially not in the growing bigger cities, but breaking and entering was not common in Tuckers Bluff. Whatever this character had in mind, Adam felt pretty sure it had something to do with Meg's trouble with the law.

At the bottom of the clinic stairs, D.J. disconnected the call to the station and turned to Adam. "Just in case this asshole is watching the street, I'll circle around from the east. You go around to the alley and go the other way up a few houses, before cutting across and coming at the café from the other direction. I'll meet you at the rear door. When you cross the street, take it easy, normal, like you were out borrowing a cup of sugar and are just heading home. Got it?"

"Got it." It didn't take long to do as instructed. When Adam made his way around, D.J. was already stationed by a thatch of shrubs kitty-corner to the property. His position allowed him a decent view of both doors. Adam looked around for signs of another person. Now that he thought about it, they didn't even know how many people were up there.

"I spotted an unfamiliar car in front of the Cut and Curl. Esther's running the plates," D.J. said calmly. "One coffee cup. Empty chocolate wrappers, not much else. I'd say whoever's up there is alone."

"You think this has something to do with the trouble Meg's in?"

"Only if the Pope's Catholic."

"Yeah. That's what I was thinking. Any idea who it is?"

D.J. shrugged. "A PI came into town last week, looking for her."

"What?" Adam almost forgot to keep his voice down.

"That's when I started calling in a few markers to keep tabs on Meg and what's going on in Dallas."

"Why didn't you tell me?"

"In case you've forgotten, I'm the police chief. You're the veterinarian. Reporting to you is not in either of our job descriptions." D.J.'s shoulders eased on a heavy breath. "Besides, how the hell was I supposed to know you'd fall hard and fast for a perfect stranger?"

Adam could argue he hadn't fallen hard or fast, but that would have been an outright lie. The other choice was to agree—for him, Meg was perfect. But, if he valued his life, Adam was better off ignoring the statement completely. For now. "Damned mess is what it is. So you think this is the PI?"

"Maybe."

"Or?" Adam looked across the darkened street to his clinic, wishing to God this was all just a nightmare.

D.J. slid his revolver from its sheath. "It could be anyone. And I mean *anyone*, so I don't want you playing like we're ten years old, pretending to be cowboys and Indians."

"I don't like the idea of you going in alone."

D.J. looked up to the second floor, and, for a brief moment, Adam could see the doubts in his brother's eyes. "One on one. Those odds are doable. Just keep your eyes peeled for Reed."

Adam nodded, but he didn't like waiting behind. Not a damn bit.

• • •

Meg wasn't sure when she'd been more scared. With every new situation this evening, her fears had escalated. At first when D.J. said he needed to speak with her on official business, then when she had learned her father was indicted and even more so at the discovery that Jonathan was trying to implicate her as well to save his sorry ass. But none of it compared to the stone-cold fear smothering her as she watched Adam and his brother huddling in the darkened corner of the café property, preparing to confront whoever had broken into her tiny apartment.

How had one man come to mean so much to her so fast? Oh, she was worried for D.J. too. He seemed to be a nice guy. The entire Farraday family was nothing but nice people. But she was more than worried about Adam. The last week she'd spent too much time glancing out the window at lunchtime, waiting, hoping he'd come in so she could have ten minutes to chat with him about nothing in particular. Each day those hopes grew stronger than the day before. Anticipation of her date had had her nearly giddy like a schoolgirl. And the reality was worth every ounce of pent-up energy. She could easily fall in love with Adam Farraday. Hell, who was she kidding? She was halfway there already.

Ringing her hands, she said a silent prayer for the men who were putting themselves at risk for her. She opened her eyes in time to see D.J. appear in the open, creeping up the stairs. Something in his hands. Dear Lord, his gun. From the corner of her eye she saw Adam make his move, trotting around to the other side. She had to place her hand on her frantic heart to stop it from beating out of her chest. This was all her fault, and these two macho brothers expected her to just stand back and watch whatever unfolded through a large screened windowpane, like a late-night movie. Only what the hell could she do to help? She looked around the room, searching for something, anything appropriate for dealing with an intruder.

All Adam needed was for her to go charging in like the unarmed too-stupid-to-live star of a bad horror movie. Never doing what she was told. Always making things worse. Putting even more people at risk. She paced across the room and back to the window. Frustration mounted. D.J. was nearly to the top of the stairs. The flashlight had turned on and disappeared again, as though maybe the intruder had slipped out of sight into her room. She could feel her skin crawl at the thought of some stranger in her private space.

Shaking away the icy fingers crawling up her back, Meg spotted something else. A car coming down the street. Slowly. With no headlights. Shit. Could this nightmare possibly get any worse?

CHAPTER EIGHTEEN

Reed Taylor parked the patrol car as close as he dared to the Silver Spurs Café. The nearly full moon would make sneaking around more challenging if anyone was watching. And he didn't doubt that more than one citizen of Tuckers Bluff was already peering through the curtains.

D.J. had texted Reed moments ago that he was at the top of the stairs, waiting for Reed to be in place. The closer he got, the easier to make out where Adam stood guard at the back door. If whoever had broken in tried to leave without using the apartment's front stairs, they'd have no choice but to enter the café in order to access the back exit. Odds of that were pretty slim, but it was good that Adam had it covered nonetheless.

Reed hunched down beside Adam. "Anything I need to know?"

"Nothing new. You probably know more than I do."

Lifting a large rock by the rear door, Reed retrieved a key, slipped it into the dead bolt and, unlocking the door, inched his way into the café's back hall, ready to climb the inside stairs. Adam was on his heels. The plan was for Reed and D.J. to come in, charging from both sides together. "You should stay here."

"Not a chance."

"We don't know what we're dealing with. You're unarmed."

"Not anymore." Adam pulled a revolver from his belt.

"Where did you get that?"

"Glove compartment. License to carry."

Reed had two choices. Delay backing up his boss by arguing with a stubborn Farraday, or moving forward and hoping to high hell Adam knew how to handle that piece in his hands. "All right. I'll cover D.J. while you cover me, and, for God's sake, don't shoot me in the back."

Adam rolled his eyes and followed Reed up the stairs. The way the officer carried on, anyone would think the men in this part of the country didn't know how to handle a gun. Each of the Farraday boys, and the sole girl, could shoot a rattlesnake from fifty feet away. If it came down to Adam needing to shoot, he would not miss.

At the top of the stairs, Adam stayed pressed to the wall, holding his breath. D.J.'s and Reed's voices called out, "Police." Doors flew open. Adam watched as the two men charged into the room, arms extended, guns pointed, scanning the far corners. "Clear," D.J. called, moving into the back. Reed approached the closed kitchen doors, flung it open and announced, "Clear." With both officers out of sight in the bedroom, Adam eased over the threshold, braced in case whoever the hell had been snooping around slipped past his brother.

Reed and D.J. came to the door, heads shaking.

"No one's here," D.J. reported.

"That doesn't make sense." Adam looked around the room, half expecting the intruder to fall from a nonexistent chandelier.

"The car was still in front of the Cut and Curl when I pulled up," Reed confirmed.

D.J.'s eyes narrowed into thin slivers as he took in the situation. "He was only out of our sight for a few seconds when we first left the clinic. If he'd made it to the car, he would be gone."

"If he left after we crossed the street, one of us would have seen him," Adam added.

"Which means—" Reed chimed in.

"Son of a bitch," D.J. and Adam echoed in unison.

Adam did an about-face and was halfway down the stairs with D.J. and Reed on his heels. The bastard had to have been hiding in the café while they positioned to enter Meg's apartment. Then, when he and Reed climbed the stairs, whoever this guy was had made his escape. Moving faster than Adam thought humanly possible, he ran straight for the front door. Shit. Unlocked. Without slowing down, already running to the clinic, he looked up the street. The car D.J. had spotted hadn't moved. Immediately his gaze shot up to his darkened living room windows. Damn it.

● ● ●

How much longer was this going to take? If, God forbid, something went wrong, Meg didn't have anyone to call. Both the police chief and his junior officer were inside her apartment. With Adam. And if she tried reaching Esther, the dispatcher, it could take hours for the neighboring police to arrive.

"Looking good tonight, Margaret."

Meg whirled around, her hand slipping from the curtain. The voice came from the direction of the front door.

"Don't look so surprised. You had to know it was me snooping around your place."

"Jonathan." Her sleazeball ex stood casually leaning against the doorjamb. Rather than being frenzied with worry over his future confinement, he looked almost … amused.

"What are you doing here?"

"I should be asking you the same question. When the more-expensive-than-God private investigator firm I hired to find you said you were working in a small-town west Texas café as a waitress, I didn't believe them. But there couldn't be two redheaded beauties like you in the great state of Texas."

She bit back the obligatory thank-you. "You didn't answer my question. What are you doing here?"

"Looking for my devoted, loving bride of course." Nothing about the way Jonathan said that put Meg at ease. "And my car."

"Car?" Even with a major jail sentence looming over him like a French guillotine, the man still fawned over that stupid sports car.

"Well, more like the million dollars hidden inside."

"A million …" What idiot runs around with a million dollars? "In cash?"

"Is there any other kind?" One brow arched north, and Meg resisted the urge to wrap her arms around herself. How had the condescension in his glare never registered with her before? Whenever he thought something she'd said had been inappropriate, that one stupid eyebrow rose up like a McDonald's arch, putting her and her alleged stupidity in its place. Though this time he was clearly the idiot. The Caribbean was filled with banks set up to hide large sums of money. They were leaving for Paris for their honeymoon. What was he planning on doing with that much cash?

"I can see those pretty little wheels turning. Did you know a million dollars fits in a grocery bag?" He nodded. "It does."

"I, uh, didn't know."

"Yes. Easy to overlook tucked into the back of the trunk. On our way to the airport I'd planned for us to make a quick deposit of sorts. A safe deposit. The one you and I opened recently."

She nodded this time. "For important papers."

"And insurance."

"Insurance?" She was lost again.

"For the future."

She wasn't stupid, but she was definitely confused. "What does a bank box have to do with insurance and the future?"

A hollow, deep, almost-crazed laugh filled the room. "You were always so easy to distract. The box is just a tool. Shouldn't you be curious about the money? Or has living in this Podunk town robbed you of what little brains you had?"

Had he really always thought her stupid? Had she missed the signs? Or had she just wanted to be in love so much that she'd turned her back on common sense? "None of this explains why you've hidden a million dollars in the car." She didn't need to ask where it had come from. That was obvious even to anyone. "And why do you want it now?"

"None of those ancient old crows were supposed to notice the details on the statement. Who knew one of them had an actuary for a grandson with a penchant to scrutinize all her investments and calculate how the math couldn't work. It should have been years, decades before it unraveled. Most of the profits are already in Grand Cayman. But, just in case, in an event such as now, I'll need additional evidence to prove to the authorities that someone else is the brains behind the operation. So someone else will need a little bit of money stashed away."

The pieces were falling into place, and she didn't like the picture. "The safety deposit box."

Jonathan tapped his nose with a single finger. "Give the girl a prize. Of course both you and your father have offshore accounts with large sums of money. The safety deposit box is just a little added prop. Sort of the cherry on the sundae."

"You're framing *me*?" That made her blood boil. When D.J. said Jonathan was offering to turn state's evidence for leniency, she thought he was stalling. It hadn't occurred to her that he would plant evidence against her.

Jonathan shrugged to show his indifference. "Both of you. All's fair in love and war. And money."

Both? Both. Then what she'd heard her daddy say really was an innocent comment. Simple direction. Relief washed over her more powerful than the fear that had kept her frozen in place.

Jonathan closed the last bit of gap between them. "But things turned around a little faster than I expected. I'll need that money now to buy my way out of here. And you"—he stood close enough for her to feel his warm breath on her face—"you are my safe passage out of here. Now where's the car?"

• • •

Adam took the stairs to his apartment two at a time. Halfway up a scream pierced the hum of blood pounding in his ears, followed by what sounded like a roaring bear. Adam knew all too well the sound of human rage. Grabbing the handrail to propel himself the rest of the way up the stairs, he shoved aside the images of a battered or broken Meg at the hands of the asshole he'd let slip through his fingers.

A muffled shout came through the door as he kicked it open. Instead of the vicious attack of a crazed man, Adam was greeted with a gut-wrenching moan and a furious woman yielding his Big Bertha Driver over a fetal ball of a man, clutching his crotch, curled at her feet.

"You sniveling bastard." Still holding the golf club over her victim like a caveman's club, Meg kicked the man while he was down. "You actually made me doubt my father. I've been hiding like a scared rabbit because of you. You tried to ruin us."

His favorite nine iron was about to again come down on her ex, or at least who Adam assumed was her ex, when Adam circled his arm around Meg's waist and scooped her aside. "I think he's had enough, Wonder Woman."

Footsteps pounded up the stairs. D.J. was the next to come into the room, his weapon drawn, Reed on his heels, along with two men Adam didn't recognize. Meg was struggling in his grasp. "Put me down."

"Not until you promise to leave the guy alone. Let the cops handle this."

D.J. was already hovering over Jonathan, yanking his hands behind his back, reading him his rights. Once D.J. had the guy on his feet, Reed holstered his weapon and turned to the two guys behind him. "We'll meet you at the station."

Both nodded and turned down the stairs without saying a word.

Still in his arms, Adam loosened his hold on Meg, giving her room to spin about. Convinced she would clobber him for pulling her off her ex, he was startled when she leaned into him, dropping her head in his shoulder. "How could I have thought I loved him?"

And how did he answer a loaded question like that? Settling one hand on her back and swirling soothing motions with the other, he kissed the top of her head.

D.J. shoved his prisoner at Reed. "Take him in. I'll be right behind you."

The officer and Jonathan followed the same path as the two

strangers.

Once they were gone, D.J. turned to his brother. "She okay?"

Adam nodded; he sure as hell hoped so. "Who are the extra guys you picked up?"

"FBI."

CHAPTER NINETEEN

Meg's head was spinning. Her world had been spiraling out of control for so long she had every right to feel dizzy. Especially around Adam. "It's late," she told him. "You should go home."

"Not that late." Sitting beside her at the police station in front of his brother's desk, Adam reminded her of a faithful dog. Or maybe a protective German shepherd. Either way, she was grateful to have him with her, even if she did feel a little off balance every time he was around.

Phone calls had been coming in and going out all night. After locking Jonathan away, the two FBI agents had remained behind closed doors with D.J. and Reed for the first hour. At first it was her word against Jonathan's, and while the agents may not have believed her ex's claims that this evening's events were all a huge misunderstanding, they didn't seem inclined to believe she was as much Jonathan's victim as her father's clients. On the bright side, no one had arrested her yet. That had to be a good sign.

For the last thirty minutes, Esther had been inside the shuttered room as well. Right now Meg hung all her hopes on the dispatcher. When the door opened, and both D.J. and Esther came out, Meg held her breath until Esther nodded and smiled.

"Okay." D.J. came into his office and took a seat behind his desk. "You're not under arrest. As a matter of fact, your father has been with the agents in Dallas for hours. Seems as soon as he left the church, he hired a few private detectives of his own to dig into Cox's background. Turns out Cox is not even his name."

"You're kidding?" A thousand thoughts bounced around in her mind. So many things made sense now. Jonathan's lack of friends, something so out of step with his charming and gregarious personality. Why he always paid cash or used her credit cards. Never wanting to talk about his childhood or family. She'd assumed he had an unhappy family life. How many other red flags had she missed?

"And this isn't the first scam he's run either," D.J. added.

"So"—Adam leaned forward in his seat—"Meg's off the hook?"

D.J. nodded and faced Meg. "Your father too. That was pretty smooth of you calling Esther when Cox showed up."

"I had her on speed dial in case you guys needed help. I'd thought about ignoring what Adam said and following you myself. Even looked around for something I could use as a weapon."

"The golf club?" D.J. asked.

Meg bobbed her head. "Pretty stupid idea. I decided keeping an eye on you and being ready to call Esther at the first sign of trouble was the smarter thing for me to do. The phone was in my hand, and the golf club was leaning by the curtain. I don't think Jonathan noticed either. The moment I recognized Jonathan's voice, I hit Dial and set the phone on the sill."

"Lucky for you," D.J. interrupted, "all incoming calls are recorded. The conversation will have to be officially transcribed, but, for now, Esther has backed up everything you and Jonathan said."

"I'd hoped she was able to hear. I was afraid we were too far away from the phone."

"The important things came in loud and clear. But this isn't over yet. Technically you're still smack-dab in the middle of an ongoing investigation."

"Will she need that lawyer?" Adam asked.

D.J. shook his head. "No. The authorities are convinced that Cox acted on his own. But Meg will have to make statements in triplicate for all the agencies dogging this case. We, of course, will have the report on tonight's incident, but Meg should make plans to return to Dallas."

"If she's in the clear," Adam asked, "why does she need to go to Dallas?"

"You mean besides that Dallas is where her life and family are?"

For a brief instant all the color drained from Adam's face. His startled expression mirrored the shocking impact D.J.'s blunt statement had on Meg too. Relief at hearing she and her father were no longer suspects faded away as reality stepped forward. Her reality. Tuckers Bluff was not her world. Nor her life.

His pointed gaze locked on Adam, D.J. continued. "Meg'll still have to answer FBI and SEC questions in their Dallas offices on all the joint assets—"

"And losses," she added. The financial fiasco Jonathan had created shriveled when compared to the bigger picture—losing what she'd found in Tuckers Bluff. Who she'd found. Something inside her shifted. Her heart sank, and an oppressive void shoved at her chest. If she made the wrong choice, the wrong decision, her new reality could be worse than all the balance sheets in the world.

• • •

The patrol car stopped in front of the diner. Much to Adam's surprise, the lights were on, and the Open for Business sign burned bright. Abbie's beige sedan was in its designated parking spot.

D.J. shifted into Park. "News of two police vehicles, two federal agents and a screaming prisoner on the streets of Tuckers Bluff in the middle of the night spreads fast. Abbie called to make sure you were all right. I may have mentioned you could probably use a friend."

A grateful gaze met D.J.'s. "That was thoughtful of you."

Thoughtful was one word for it. Unfortunately it also didn't make getting a few minutes alone with Meg to talk any easier. Pretty soon half the town would be awake and gathering at the café, and Adam still had no idea if Meg would be returning to Dallas sooner or later. For a visit or for good. The latter words had icy fingers clamping tightly around his heart. His dad had always told his sons that, the minute he'd laid eyes on Helen Callahan, his whole world had come to a stop. In the next minute when Adam's mom had pinned his dad with her beautiful Irish green eyes and told Sean Patrick O'Brien to get his muddy boots off her clean floor, he'd fallen Stetson over heels in love with her. It had taken his father the next six months to convince her of what he'd known in only five minutes—that they were meant to be together.

If what Adam feared was true, he might not have five minutes to convince Meg to give him a chance, never mind six months.

They'd barely stepped from the car when Abbie came flying out the café door and racing up to Meg and drew her into a motherly hug. "I have been so worried. I knew there was a no-good bastard in your life. I just knew it."

A caustic chuckle escaped past Meg's lips. "Don't forget *thieving*."

Abbie slid her arm down Meg's side, turning her toward the café. The two walked side by side, like a Hallmark best friends' card. "This calls for some of my special hot chocolate."

"I don't think so."

"With Baileys," Abbie added with a smile, then called over her shoulder, "You didn't hear that PC Farraday."

Standing beside him, D.J. laughed quietly. "Like I don't know about her 'special' stash. I need to get back to the mountain of paperwork. You going to be okay?"

Adam nodded, even though he wasn't all too sure.

"Are you just going to stand here in the parking lot?"

Dragging his gaze away from the two women crossing into the café, Adam faced his brother, the sudden turn of events robbing him of coherent thought.

"Oh, for Christ's sake. If you want her, go after her." Shaking his head, D.J. spun about and climbed into his car, mumbling something about "how the mighty have fallen."

Adam had not a clue what to do now, but his brother was right about one thing. Revelation wouldn't come by standing alone outside. By the time he'd walked inside, Meg was sitting at a booth, talking on the phone.

His gaze caught Abbie's. Working behind the counter, she bobbed her head and, tipping her head in Meg's direction, urged him to join her.

"Yes, Daddy. I'm sorry."

"If you'd taken the time to call me, I could have told you what was going on, Margaret Colleen." Her father spoke so loudly through the phone that, even across the café, Abbie could probably hear him.

"I wanted to protect you."

"Baby girl, don't you ever run off, and cut your mother and me out of your troubles again. Do you hear me?"

"Yes, Daddy."

Adam sat quietly as she explained to her father about the car, the bill, the lack of funds and earning her keep at the café. Every so often her sorrowful eyes lifted to meet his and then looked down again to the fork she spun between her fingers.

"I'll be home soon, Daddy. Yes. I promise."

After a few more words of love and support, Meg disconnected the call.

"Are you all right?" Adam asked.

"Still a little stunned, I guess."

Abbie came over and set two mugs of steaming hot cocoa in front of them. "You sip that slowly. I'm not nearly as good a cook as Frank, but I can manage to scramble a few eggs. You drink that down to settle your nerves, then you'll put some food in your stomach. No one ever made smart decisions on an empty stomach."

Adam screwed up his courage. Not sure he wanted to hear the answer. "Now what happens?"

"I go home." She stared into the mug.

Even though she couldn't see him, Adam nodded, took a sip, and then pressed on. "Coming back?"

This time she raised her gaze to meet his. "I don't know. I honestly don't know."

CHAPTER TWENTY

"You can't keep moping around the house." Meg's mom stood in the bedroom doorway, her hands fisted on her hips. "I know things look pretty bleak, but your father and the authorities have uncovered at least two overseas bank accounts and are still digging up where Jonathan hid the rest of the money stolen from his clients' accounts. There'll be a loss but not as bad as it could be if this had gone on for years."

Meg nodded. She was glad the feds had also recovered the money hidden in the trunk and that her father's clients would be able to recoup a good portion of their investment, but she really didn't feel like talking about it.

"Margaret Colleen." Her mother stomped into the room and stopped at her bedside. "It's time to move on. Jonathan Cox, or whatever his name is, is not worth all this brooding."

On the computer screen, Meg scanned the details of the real estate contract in front of her. The first thing she'd done was hire a Realtor to put the condo on the market, and, in less than twenty-four hours, she had multiple offers. Bless the booming Dallas real estate market. Even though she'd lost some money selling the Ferrari, her stellar diamond ring and other trappings Jonathan had bought on her credit—like their Paris, France, honeymoon—the bidding war price for the condo looked to put her in the black again. Not by much but it was nothing to sneeze at.

"Did you hear me, young lady?" Scowling, her mother crossed her arms in frustration. Any minute now she was bound to start tapping her toe.

"I'm not moping, Mom. I'm taking care of business." And maybe wondering for the billionth time what Adam was doing at this same moment.

Her laptop dinged with an instant message. From Abbie. That woman had been a great boss, and, since the Jonathan debacle had come to a head, she'd become an even better friend. Happy for the distraction, Meg clacked away at the keyboard.

ABBIE: Did you hear about Myrtle Yantz?

MEG: No. What?

ABBIE: Grandbaby number two is on the way. She's decided she's not coming back to Tuckers Bluff.

"What kind of business?" her mother asked.

ABBIE: Her house just went on the market.

Really? Meg looked at the offer price on the condo. The real estate markets in Dallas and Tuckers Bluff were worlds apart. Planets apart.

"Well?" her mother repeated.

ABBIE: Can't imagine who would want to buy that big old thing. Needs so much work.

As the glimmer of an idea took root, a smile tugged at one side of Meg's mouth, spreading the grin to the other side of her lips until the fully formed idea had her tossing aside her laptop and springing from bed.

"The best kind of business, Mom." Meg kissed her mother on the cheek and whizzed around her, repeating over her shoulder. "The absolute best."

● ● ●

Behind his desk, pen in hand, Adam made a futile effort to finish his paperwork. Lately, working on the animals was the only time he was able to stay on task. At his desk or helping out at the ranch, with a will of its own, his mind kept circling back to Meg. And over her, under her or just about any place two people could fit. Not for the first time he considered how impossible it would be to turn his life upside down and follow the woman to Dallas.

"It works better if you actually put the pen to the page." Becky came into the room and dropped into one of the two chairs flanking his desk.

"I know."

"Have you spoken with her?"

There was no need to ask who *her* was. He and Becky had already had this conversation. He shook his head. There was also no point in mentioning how many times he'd picked up the phone to call Meg. Say hello. Just hello. And then, deciding a casual chat would never be enough, set aside the phone.

"Hey, did you hear?" Kelly came bouncing through the doorway. "Someone bought Myrtle's place."

Becky's whole face scrunched up. "You're kidding?"

"Nope." Kelly dropped into the second chair. "Realtor just stuck the Sold banner on the sign. Said a cash offer came in and closed in less than a week. Who would want that rambling old place badly enough to be in such a hurry?"

"I don't know." Adam held up his pen. "But, if you ladies didn't notice, I have work to do."

"No one around here surely," Becky answered, ignoring her boss.

"Wonder what they'll do with it?" Kelly inched forward in her seat in a weak effort to stand and return to work.

Becky shrugged. The sound of a car pulling into a parking spot in front of the clinic caught everyone's attention.

"We don't have any more appointments scheduled, do we?" Adam asked.

The two women across from him shook their heads, both craning their necks to see out

the window. Becky was the first one to make out the visitor, her eyes rounded like a full moon. "Holy shit." She sprang to her feet and bolted out the door.

Pushing to her feet, Kelly squinted out the window. "Well, I'll be …"

"What?" A car door slammed, but Adam didn't turn around fast enough to see the passenger. By the time he'd faced the chairs by his desk, both his employees were gone, kicking up a wind on their way out the door.

"What the hell?" Only an emergency could have both of those girls running like the barn was on fire. On his feet, he was halfway to the hall when, dressed in a creamy white sleeveless dress, his redheaded angel came to a halt in his doorway.

"There's this dog …" Meg's words came out soft and slow.

The familiar words from weeks ago mixed with the sultry timbre of her voice had his heart galloping and all his senses pinging on high alert. "Dog?"

"I've been waiting for daylight. I have to find him." She inched forward.

Suddenly parched, his mouth struggled to form words. "Could be you just saw a coyote?"

She shook her head. "Coyote's in Dallas." Glassy, hopeful eyes remained trained on his.

"I could help you find him." Adam eased forward, allowing himself the hope or feeding the delusion she was here for him, but he wouldn't, couldn't, hold back now.

"He's a cagey fellow. Finding him could take a while." She closed the distance between them.

Gently Adam let his hands fall on her waist. "Then you'll have to stay put till we can find him."

Nodding, a tentative smile touched her lips. "I've bought Myrtle's house. Thought it would make a wonderful bed-and-breakfast."

"Smart, beautiful, loves animals and she cooks too." He hoped to hell his tone succeeded in hiding just how damn nervous he was.

"Well"—her smile grew stronger, steadier, brighter—"there may be a few challenges in my plans."

Tied together, adrenaline and anticipation soared. This was it. Time to cut to the chase. "And what are those plans, Meg?"

The last few inches between them disappeared, Meg's arms wound around his neck, drawing his head down. Bringing his face to hers, she captured his mouth in a searing kiss. Coherent thought slipped away, anticipation shoved aside by joy and pleasure. She was here, with him, and, if he had anything to say about it, she was never leaving Tuckers Bluff again without him.

Filled with wanting and longing and an all-consuming need to be one in body and soul with his redheaded angel, only one thing was missing. Dragging away his mouth, he lightly touched one corner of her lips, then the other. Her soft mewl of pleasure and her warm fingertips swirling at his nape made pulling back even harder, but he had to. He had to be clear. Ignoring the rush of arousal thrumming through his veins, he took a deep calming breath. His lips a breath away from hers, he crossed the last barrier. "I love you, Margaret Colleen O'Brien."

Her lips curved against his, her hot breath mercilessly teasing his senses. "God, I hoped I wasn't the only one. I love you, Adam Farraday."

Never had any words sounded so sweet. Drawing her in, his mouth crashed against hers. Having this woman in his arms forever would not be long enough.

Shoes clacking a soft tattoo on the tile hallway floor grew louder, then came to a nearby halt. "Your aunt is ... oops."

"Oops, what?" Eileen Callahan asked on Becky's heels, looking up and stopping short. "Oh ... Well." Her face lit in a brilliant smile. "About damn time. One down, only six to go."

EPILOGUE

"**W**ill you two cut it out? That wallpaper isn't coming down on its own."

Brooks turned his back on Meg and his brother. Watching the two of them kissing and cooing like a pair of besotted teens was getting a tad uncomfortable. Wetting down another swath of wall, Brooks took the four-inch putty knife and, putting all his pent-up frustrations into the job, continued his efforts at peeling one hundred years of wallpaper off the parlor's east wall.

For just about a month the family had been spending a few hours here or there—and the better part of Saturdays and Sundays—ripping and peeling off wallpaper, replacing rotted studs and floorboards, sanding, scraping, crawling, piping. Pretty much doing just about anything imaginable to whip this old Victorian back into shape.

"Again"—this time Aunt Eileen's voice huffed—"I'd swear you were the first couple to ever get engaged." Shaking her head, their aunt stomped off.

"One little kiss," Adam muttered, pulling away from his new fiancée and returning his attention to scraping the soaked walls.

"One?" D.J. called from across the hall.

"Little?" Brooks faced his eldest brother again. "I was seriously thinking of tossing a bucket of water on you two. You know, to save the house from burning down."

"Ha, ha," Adam shot back.

Meg, on the other hand, sauntered over to her future brother-in-law, inched up on tiptoe and offered Brooks a chaste peck on the cheek. "Thank you for worrying about my house."

There was no playing upset with Meg around. For years the

brothers had teased and roughhoused, but Meg had a way of chasing away all the bluster. "Anytime."

"Watch it. She's taken." Adam pretended offense.

As if there wasn't a single person in town who didn't already know that.

"Who's got the hammer?" Their father joined them in the parlor. "My hammer."

"This one?" Adam held out the framing hammer his father always used.

"Yes, that one." Shaking his head, the family patriarch returned to his demolition project of the first-floor powder room. Originally installed in a corner under the stairs, Meg had decided—for a formal bed-and-breakfast—something a little more spacious would be required. So Dad was absorbing the old coat closet into the space.

"Lunch is served," Eileen called from the new kitchen.

"Every time I walk in here, it takes my breath away." Meg scanned the newly remodeled room. Commercial-grade appliances, quartz countertops, new Shaker cabinets and an island big enough to seat every member of the Farraday clan. "This is fabulous."

"Heart of the home and all that." D.J. grabbed a tortilla chip and scooped up a glob of guacamole. "Always the best, Aunt Eileen."

Adam sidled up to Meg and, holding an empty plate in one hand, slid the other around her waist, whispered something only Meg would hear and gently kissed her temple. The gesture wasn't grand or life-altering or earth-shattering, and yet the depth of emotions passing between him and his future bride kicked Brooks hard in his breadbasket. Until now he hadn't given love and marriage and a family of his own any thought. Maybe it was time to rethink his policy of not dating locals.

Then again, Adam hadn't changed the steadfast Farraday rule. He'd simply found his destiny stranded in the middle of nowhere. Brooks shook his head. No way would he get that lucky. What were the odds of finding another woman on the side of the road?

Enjoy an excerpt from

Brooks

Brooks Farraday stripped off his surgical gloves and flung them across the room. He'd done everything he could to stabilize the eighty-year-old woman, but Sam had waited too long to bring Liza in. With the closest major medical facility capable of doing emergency heart surgery over an hour away, there wasn't a damn thing more Brooks could have done. Frustration clawed at him as he crossed the room, picked the gloves off the floor, and slammed them into the bin. Damn, he hated days like this.

The last thing he wanted was to face Sam. Only last week the whole town had turned out for their sixtieth wedding anniversary. Brooks' storefront set up here was small: a waiting room, a converted kitchen for a lab, an oversized closet that passed for his office and two exam rooms. The corridors of the Taj Mahal wouldn't have been long enough of a walk to forestall the inevitable. Standing in a huddle, Sam and the handful of his and Liza's eight children and their spouses who still lived in or near town stared up at him. No matter how hard Brooks tried through the years to void his expression of any emotion, the loss had to have shown. Two of the daughters burst into tears.

"I'm so sorry," he said.

Gray haired and of wiry build, Sam ducked his chin, "You done all you could. I know that. Me and Liza thank you for that much." The old man turned and walked out the door before Brooks could offer to let him say his last goodbyes.

"We knew this day was coming, Brooks. Mom's heart has been threatening her for almost a decade." Sam and Liza's oldest son gave Brooks a pat on the arm, shifted his gaze across the small room, and then turned away. "I'd better catch up with Dad."

In a whirlwind of motion the remaining siblings offered some words before chasing after their father.

Nora Brown, his RN, came up behind him. "I've called Andy

at the funeral home. He's on his way over."

Brooks bowed his head. He was supposed to save lives.

"Also, Meg called, wanted to remind you about her friend. She suggested tonight would be a good night to join them for supper."

Letting his eyes fall shut, he blew out a tired breath. He was not up to socializing.

"She also said to tell you Friday night would be good too if you prefer."

His future sister-in-law seemed able to read his mind from across town even before he knew what he was thinking. Heaven help his brother Adam. Anticipating the arrival of her college friend for the wedding, Meg had been bouncing around for days like a little girl with a new jump rope. But then yesterday she'd called him worried about her friend's odd behavior and asked Brooks to stop by for dinner and see if he noticed it too. He nodded at Nora waiting patiently for a response. "Thanks. I'll give her a—"

The front door burst open and Paul Brady came rushing through. "It's time, doc. Betty Sue, she's in the car. Says she ain't moving. Sent me to come get you."

Brooks turned on his heel, shouting over his shoulder, "How long has she been having contractions?"

"Don't know. But the pains are coming five minutes apart."

Trotting toward the car tilting awkwardly with one wheel on the curb, Brooks almost smiled at the crazed parking job. *First time parents.*

The expectant father beat him to the vehicle, yanking the passenger door open.

"Hey, doc," Betty Sue said through clenched teeth.

"How's it going? Think we can get you inside?"

Betty Sue panted through a contraction, nodding her head, and then let out a long deep breath. "What I really want is to push, but if you'll give me a hand." She stuck out her arm and leaned forward. "With Ricky Ricardo here helping I wasn't sure we'd make it."

This time Brooks did chuckle at the *I Love Lucy* reference. He had no trouble envisioning Paul Brady scattering about like Ricky Ricardo had when his TV son was born. "At least he didn't leave you behind," Brooks said through a lazy smile as he eased his arm around Betty Sue and hefted her onto her feet. Only then did he catch the glare she shot her husband's way. "He didn't?"

"He did. Halfway to the road before he turned around to get me." Betty Sue made it as far as the threshold before doubling over with another contraction.

"Breathe," Brooks encouraged. By his estimation her contractions were only two or three minutes apart. If they didn't hurry up and get her settled in, he might very well be delivering this baby on the sidewalk. "How long have you been in labor?"

The very pregnant woman blew out another deep breath. "Woke up around five this morning with some of those Braxton Hicks contractions, but by around seven I realized they were real labor pains. Not too close. Prepared myself for a long day." She moved forward into the waiting room. "But about an hour ago they started coming really fast."

"Well, it looks like, for a first baby, Paul Junior is in a hurry."

Andy from the funeral home came through the open door and stopped short. He had the good sense to wait until Brooks and his patient were past the first exam room before looking to Nora for answers.

"Room one," was all Nora said.

In the second exam room, Brooks and Paul settled Betty Sue onto the bed. Slightly larger than exam room one with a nice bed and some homey decorations nearby, this space doubled as a birthing room. Behind them, Nora came in and set up the oxygen. Just in case.

"Let me take a look." As Brooks had expected, Betty Sue was fully dilated and effaced. Baby Paul was ready to make his entrance. "I know you want to push, but I need a few more seconds here."

Panting through another contraction Betty Sue nodded and stretched her hand out for her husband. In what proved to be a routine, though speedy, delivery, in only fifteen minutes Paul Brady Junior slid into the world.

"You ready to hold your son?" Brooks asked Betty Sue.

With a smile brighter than a kid at Christmas, the new mother stretched out her arms. Paul kissed his wife's forehead and then did the same to the top of the tiny boy's head.

"We'll have to weigh him and do a couple of standard tests, but that can wait a few minutes for you three to get acquainted." Brooks stepped back, his gaze on the newborn infant. Brooks' heart was lighter. The circle of life. "Welcome to the world, young man. Welcome to the world."

● ● ●

"I'll see your five and raise you five." Antoinette Castelano Bennett tossed a couple of chips into the growing pile. When she'd envisioned coming to west Texas to visit her college roommate before her wedding, playing poker with the geriatric crowd wasn't exactly the pastime she'd pictured.

"I'm out." Dorothy Wilson, a sweet and friendly older lady set her cards face down on the table.

"Me too." Sally May, an attractive woman with salt and pepper hair in a simple French twist and a German shepherd curled up at her feet set her cards down with a sigh.

"Guess that leaves me." Eileen Callahan, the matriarch of the family Toni's friend was marrying into, had a grin as wide as the west Texas horizon. Adding more chips to the pot with one hand, she laid her five cards out, face up, with the other. "Three aces."

The last member of the group, Ruth Ann, let out a frustrated groan. A short, very thin woman with long gray hair clipped in a sloppy pony tail, wearing jeans and a blue long sleeve shirt, she reminded Toni of everything she would have pictured a rancher's wife to be. Except instead of talking about cattle or chickens, every other sentence had something to do with her recent bunion surgery. "That leaves me out. Got two pair, king high."

Which left only Toni holding cards. Remembering what her grandmother used to say, Lucky in cards unlucky in love, she wasn't feeling very triumphant. "Sorry ladies. Full house. Three queens over a pair of tens."

"I'm going to take a walk to the ladies room." Sally May pushed to her feet. "Maybe it will change my luck."

Next to deal, Eileen gathered the cards from the table. "So tell us more about this traveling husband of yours?"

Separating the winning till into appropriate colored stacks, Toni considered what to say. The call that had sent her husband packing his bag and rushing to Logan airport for a flight to one of those *Stan* countries had been an unexpected gift. William never did off shore sites any more, but when the engineer assigned for this project suffered a massive heart attack on his way to the airport, the partners had scrambled for a replacement project manager and William had been the only person with enough flexibility and skill to go.

Remembering the harrowing twenty-minute rush had her gripping her chips more tightly.

"Damn it, Antoinette. There's too much starch in my shirts. Again."

"I'm sorry." She hated ironing shirts. *"Maybe this one will be—"*

William snatched the shirt out of her hand and slammed it into his suitcase. "I don't want to wear that shirt on the plane."

Toni bounced back from his reach. She wasn't making that mistake again.

"If that dumb knothead at the dry cleaners can get the starch right there's no reason you can't. You don't have to be a Rhodes Scholar to iron a shirt."

"Toni?" Eileen's hands had stilled in mid shuffle, her brows pinched with concern.

"Sorry, my mind wandered. Yes. William doesn't travel much

anymore. He's very protective of me. Doesn't like to be away from me at all, but he didn't have any choice this time."

"Well it was very fortuitous that his extended trip coincided with my wedding, even if I had to use my best debate skills to get you to come and visit now instead of only for the wedding weekend." Meg O'Brien—soon to be Farraday—stood at Toni's side, a coffeepot in hand. "Sounds like he turned out to be a very loving husband."

"Yes. Loving." Under the table Toni clenched her hands together, forced the plastic I'm so happily married smile she always used in public and pushed aside her husband's last words on his way out the door.

"I don't know how reliable the satellites are in that God forsaken temporary engineering camp. For God's sake don't forget to charge your phone. Better yet, stay close to home. In that armpit of a country, who knows what I might need ..."

She knew what close to home meant. Not that it would be hard to do. Where did she have to go?

"My mother will be back from her cruise in a few weeks. When she returns, I'll arrange for you to stay with her while I'm gone." His gaze darted about the pristine condo. "I'll be back much sooner than three months if I have anything to say about it. That mudhole corner of the world is no place for a man like me."

She nodded. Not sure what he expected her to do next. If this would be the time he'd want her to hand him the rest of his things to make packing go faster, or would this be when nothing she did would be right. The outburst over the shirt had her thinking she'd be better off waiting for instructions. Maybe.

"Meg is right." Eileen dealt the cards. "It's always nice to have friends visit. And she tells me you're quite the cook too? She needs some fattening up. Working here every morning and fixing up that old house the rest of the time, she's wearing herself to a skeleton. Which reminds me." Sorting her hand, Eileen looked over her shoulder at Meg. "I've almost got the drapes done for the old parlor. These are the last of the curtains."

"Sound like time for a decorating party." Sally May picked up her cards.

Eileen nodded. "It's been fun bringing that old house back to life."

From what Meg had told Toni, the Farraday clan had spent more time putting around the old Victorian than they had at their own homes and Meg seemed to love every minute of suddenly being part of a large tight knit family. Toni couldn't imagine. Whenever her husband's family descended on Boston, helpful wasn't the first word that came to mind.

"Sounds good." A customer across the café waved Meg down and she took off in their direction.

When Toni married William and settled in the bustling heart of Boston's Back Bay she thought she'd won the lottery. Watching Meg smile and flutter from table to table, glowing from the inside out, Toni wondered if she'd ever been that happy. Barely glancing at her cards, Toni tossed the hand onto the table. "I think I'm going to sit this one out. Could use a little fresh air."

"Oh good." Ruth Ann sprang up laughing. "I'll sit in the hot seat while she's gone."

Meg came hurrying back to the table. "You ready to go? I've got about another half hour till Shannon comes in."

"I was just going to stretch my legs, but maybe a nice walk home would be better."

Meg studied her a little longer than she'd have liked. "Good idea. Back door is unlocked. I'll get home as soon as I can."

"No hurry."

"Can you find your way?"

Toni almost laughed. The town wasn't that big and what there was of it had been built out in a basic grid. It might take her all of fifteen minutes to walk down Main Street and then turn up onto Meg's block. "I'll be fine."

"Will we see you for Saturday's card game?" Dorothy Wilson looked up. "Nora comes on Saturdays."

"I don't know. Depends on how much work there is to be

done at Meg's," Toni said.

"Work my foot." Meg winked at her friend. "Saturday we're heading to Abilene. I've got some more shopping to do."

"I'm in." Toni smiled at her friend and realized for the first time in a very long time she was doing an awful lot of heartfelt smiling.

Though she'd seen the main street shops driving through town before, she took her time now, glancing at the people coming and going, spending an extra minute or two looking at the window displays. The inside of the Cut and Curl looked like it hadn't changed much since the day it was built. In a line along the back wall were several of the old-fashioned massive hair dryers. Even now, two women sat side by side flipping through magazines.

When Toni pictured west Texas she had a vision of Clint Eastwood chasing cows down a dirt road flanked by wooden sidewalks. She hadn't pictured Mayberry.

About to turn the corner up Meg's street, a muffled woof caught her attention. Still too far from the residential part of the block for there to be a nearby yard with a dog, she paused and looked around. Nothing. A few more steps and she heard it again, only this time the woof had more of a whine to it. Where was it coming from?

Taking her time to scan the area, Toni inched slowly forward, listening carefully. And there it was again, a little louder and coming from across the street. Almost willing the animal to show itself, she stepped off the curb. Movement in the shrubs alongside a boarded up house told her she was heading in the right direction when a black muzzle appeared, followed by a furry body and at last a drooping tale. All walking in her direction. With a limp.

For a short second she'd thought it might have been Sally May's German shepherd, but then realized this dog was more gray than tan, and a bit shorter than the eighty pound shepherd. "Oh sweetie." Nearly to the other side of the street, she squatted down for the dog to close the gap between them. "What happened?"

Without any sign of fear or hesitation, the dog walked right up to her and nuzzled his head into her outstretched hand.

"Well you're a friendly fella, aren't you?"

The tail gave a brief swish as Toni scratched behind the dog's ear, then ran her other hand down the length of him. Or her. No collar. No tangles of fur. Thin but not skeletal. The dog had either been on its own a while and knew how to care for itself, or had a miserly master. When she let her hand glide gently over the leg the dog seemed to favor, the friendly pup let out a small whine.

"Okay, looks like we're going to have to find you a vet. I just happen to know where there's a very good one."

The dog shifted and rubbed against her, eating up all the attention. She understood exactly how the poor dog felt. Loneliness sucked.

MEET CHRIS

USA TODAY Bestselling Author of more than a dozen contemporary novels, including the award winning *Champagne Sisterhood*, Chris Keniston lives in suburban Dallas with her husband, two human children, and two canine children. Though she loves her puppies equally, she admits being especially attached to her German Shepherd rescue. After all, even dogs deserve a happily ever after.

More on Chris and her books can be found at
www.chriskeniston.com

Follow Chris on Facebook at ChrisKenistonAuthor
or on Twitter @ckenistonauthor

Questions? Comments?
I would love to hear from you.
You can reach me at chris@chriskeniston.com